AFRICAN
SHORT STORIES

AFRICAN/AMERICAN LIBRARY
General Editor Charles R. Larson

A continuing series of works of literary excellence by
black writers in the United States, Africa and the Caribbean.

AFRICAN SHORT STORIES

A COLLECTION OF
CONTEMPORARY AFRICAN WRITING

Edited and with an Introduction by
CHARLES R. LARSON

Collier Books

The Macmillan Company
866 Third Avenue, New York, N.Y. 10022
Library of Congress Catalog Card Number: 70-109450

First Printing

Printed in the United States of America

ACKNOWLEDGMENTS

*For permission to reprint the stories in this collection, grateful
acknowledgment is made to the following:*
Ellen Conroy Kennedy and Presence Africaine for "Black Girl,"
by Sembene Ousmane, from *Voltaigue*, and for "Sarzan," by Birago Diop, from *Les Contes D'Amadou Koumba*; Abioseh Nicol,
for "The Truly Married Woman," from *The Truly Married
Woman and Other Stories*, published by the Oxford University
Press; James Matthews for "The Party," from *Quartet: New
Voices From South Africa*, by Richard Rive, Copyright © 1963
by Crown Publishers, Inc., used by permission; Amos Tutuola
for "The Complete Gentleman," from *The Palm-Wine Drinkard*, reprinted by permission of Faber and Faber Ltd.; Barbara
Kimenye for "The Winner," from *Kalasanda*, published by the
Oxford University Press (Three Crowns Series); Sylvian Bemba
for "The Dark Room," from *African Writing Today*, published
by Penguin Books Ltd.; Alex La Guma for "A Matter of Taste,"
published by Heinemann Educational Books; Cameron Duodu
for "The Tax Dodger"; James Ngugi for "A Meeting in the
Dark"; Nuwa Sentongo for "Mulyankota"; Ezekiel Mphahlele
for "Mrs. Plum," published by the East African Publishing
House in 1967.

In Memory of My *Mother*

Contents

INTRODUCTION

In Africa, the modern short story falls into two patterns quite similar to what we are familiar with in the United States. There is, on the one hand, a market and a reading audience similar to that of the pulp magazines here in the West. *Drum* (South African and West African editions) and *Spear* (Nigeria) are typical of this kind of African publication. There is also a literary audience for the type of writing found in the more sophisticated publications such as *Black Orpheus* (Nigeria), *Transition* (Uganda), *The Classic* (South Africa), etc. The result is that, in spite of its youth (hardly more than twenty years), the modern short story in Africa has already established two widely differentiated reading audiences.

There is also a third "type" of story which many people consider to be much more typically African: the traditional oral tale which is rooted in folklore and mythology and passed down from generation to generation. Although this type of literature is still very much alive today, with the possible exceptions of Amos Tutuola and Nuwa Sentongo, it is something we are not concerned with in this present collection of modern African short stories. One further difference between the traditional African tale and the modern African short story that needs to be mentioned, however, is the use of language. All of the short stories in this present collection were written originally in English or French, while the traditional tale was and is still being told in any one of several hundred African vernacular languages and dialects.

It is the modern short story which we are concerned with here, however, and the dichotomy of the two reading audiences has indeed determined the selection of the twelve stories in this collection. I have purposely omitted those stories (and therefore those writers) who have written almost exclusively for the African commercial magazines, and chosen, instead, those more artistically designed pieces which in some ways are closer to Western convention. This choice has meant, of course, that certain African writers famous in their own countries, such as the Nigerian Cyprian Ekwensi, have had to be omitted from this volume. Some readers already familiar with contemporary African fiction will perhaps say that this present collection is not a faithful picture of African writing. With this I agree in part, but at the same time argue that were I editing a collection of American short stories for overseas distribution, there would be no doubt in my mind whether to include the American pulp writers or not.

Writing markets being what they are throughout much of the world, it is logical that individual publications cater to a certain type of reading audience; and formula fiction is pretty much what we are likely to find if we read any of the more commercial African publications. (To a certain extent, it can be argued that the African "pulp" writers are much more Western than their counterparts who publish in the literary magazines, since a great amount of African "pulp" fiction tends to be grounded rather traditionally in the school of Poe and O'Henry.) In an article written a number of years ago, Tom Hopkinson, a one-time editor of the South African publication *Drum*, described the kind of fiction frequently submitted to that publication:

> One of the first things I stumbled across in the *Drum* office after taking over was a filing cabinet stuffed with stories sent in for a Short Story Competition, launched some fifteen months before and seem-

ingly forgotten. Partly for interest—and partly because I have a fussy disposition and like to see everything in order—I read the stories through. There were half a dozen love stories, one or two nature stories about personalized lions and leopards clearly imitated from the "Wild Animal School" of English and American magazines, but the enormous majority were fantasies of ferocity, centering either around gangster life in the townships or that legitimized outlet for violence—the boxing ring. But in these mere boxing had seldom satisfied the writer, and the fight would be continued elsewhere in more deadly form. The theme of almost all, in one form or another, was destruction.

Lewis Nkosi, in his collection of essays, *Home and Exile*, has also commented on the *Drum*-style short story, referring to it as "sleazier prose" than that found in other periodicals.

In spite of the readership associated with *Drum* (at least at the time of its origins), the magazine's significance should not be negated. South Africa has probably produced more skilled short story writers than any other country on the continent, and *Drum*'s influence as a catalyst and as a source of encouragement for a great many younger writers should not be overlooked. *Drum* came into existence in 1950 and one of the earliest South African writers who worked for the magazine (which was a general periodical only partly devoted to fiction) was Ezekiel Mphahlele, who has said in his excellent work, *The African Image*, that the appearance of *Drum* "excited enormous writing activity in the form of the short story and sketches through the medium of English."

Mphahlele has also referred to *Drum* fiction as "escapist short stories," noting too that he feels they are a "passing stage." It is in *The African Image*, furthermore, that we find an explanation for the abundance of excellent short stories which have been penned by South African writers. Mphahlele writes:

It is not easy for the oppressed African to organize himself for the writing of a novel unless he produces the kind that panders to European "supremacy." The short story strikes swiftly and drives home a point with economy of language and time. The short story in such a multi-racial setting, in my own experience, goes through three stages: the romantic-escapist; the protest short story; and the ironic, which is the meeting point between protest and acceptance.

In all three of the short stories by South African writers included in this collection (Mphahlele, La Guma, and Matthews), protest is a factor, yet, as we can clearly see (perhaps best in Mphahlele's own story, "Mrs. Plum"), the ironic level takes priority to that of the strict polemic.

To a large extent protest is missing in short stories from West and East Africa—at least protest resulting from a multi-racial situation. There is still the ironic problem of the clash of cultures between Africa and the West which is undoubtedly the most common theme of all African fiction—the novel and the short story included. Whether this be from exposure to Western religion, as in the case of Abioseh Nicol's humorous story, "The Truly Married Woman"; or to education, as in Cameron Duodo's "The Tax Dodger" and James Ngugi's "A Meeting in the Dark"; or a direct exposure to Europe itself, as in Birago Diop's "Sarzan," Sembene Ousmane's "Black Girl," or Sylvain Bemba's "The Dark Room," the African/West clash is ubiquitously present. Only in Amos Tutuola's "The Complete Gentleman" and Nuwa Sentongo's "Mulyankota" does the theme appear to be missing, and this is undoubtedly because these two stories rely heavily on oral tradition and are much less Westernized.

The term "Westernized" has been used several times here, and yet the expression is particularly annoying to many Africanists. My use of the term has been intentional, however, because my prime objective in editing this collection of African short stories has been to show the non-African reader exactly what is happening to the short story in Africa. My own belief is that the current generation of African writers is doing exciting things to the art form known as the short story. As a couple of examples I mention only Amos Tutuola's "The Complete Gentleman" for its haunting mixture of language and folklore, and Birago Diop's "Sarzan" for its brilliant use of poetry and prose (reminiscent in some ways of the black American writer, Jean Toomer, and his masterpiece, *Cane*). The reader can make the other discoveries for himself, discoveries which by now should be fairly obvious: the African writer has not been wholly content to leave the short story the way he found it. Rather, as with other forms of African writing, he has stretched it a bit by injecting a healthy dose of his own cultural and aesthetic values into a traditional Western genre and created in the process a frequently new and radically different form.

The twelve short stories in this volume for the most part have previously been unavailable in collections or anthologies of African writing published in the United States. In several cases I have simply taken what I have considered to be the best story from a volume of short stories by an individual African writer already published in England or Africa—Abioseh Nicol's "The Truly Married Woman" (Oxford University Press), for example. Or Ezekiel Mphahlele's "Mrs. Plum" from his collection *In Corner B*, published by the East African Publishing House. Other stories have been collected from an occasional African or European periodical, such as Cameron Duodu's "The Tax Dodger," which originally appeared in the Ghanaian publication, *Okyeame*. Two of the stories in this collection ("Black Girl" and "Sarzan") have been especially translated by Ellen Conroy Kennedy, who is well known not only as a translator but also as an authority on French African writing. Nuwa Sentongo's spoof on African writing, "Mulyankota," is published here for the first time. And, lastly, in the case of Amos Tutuola, I have relied on an excerpt from a longer work, since Tutuola's "novels" are constructed of shorter tales, linked by a common pursuit.

CHARLES R. LARSON

BLACK GIRL

Sembene Ousmane

Translated from the French by Ellen Conroy Kennedy

"Black Girl" ("La Noire de . . .") is from Sembene Ousmane's collection of short stories, *Voltaique*, published in 1962. A movie version of the story was filmed by the author several years ago and shown at the First World Festival of Negro Arts in Dakar in 1966. Ousmane, who is Senegalese, is the author of several novels, including *Le Docker Noir* (1956); *Les Bouts de Bois de Dieu* (1960), published in the United States as *God's Bits of Wood*; and *L'Harmattan* (1964).

It was the morning of the 23rd of June in the year of our Lord nineteen hundred fifty-eight. At Antibes, along the Riviera, neither the fate of the French Republic, nor the future of Algeria nor the state of the colonial territories preoccupied those who swarmed across the beaches below La Croisette.

Above, on the road leading to the Hermitage, two old-style Citroëns, one behind the other, were moving up the mountain. They stopped and several men quickly got out, rushing down the gravel walk toward a house on which a worn sign spelled out "Villa of Green Happiness." The men were the police chief of the town of Grasse, a medical officer, and two police inspectors from Antibes, flanked by officers in uniform.

There was nothing green about the Villa of Green Happiness except its name. The garden was kept in the

French manner, the walks covered with gravel, set off by a couple of palm trees with drooping fronds. The Chief looked closely at the house, his eyes stopping at the third window, the broken glass, the ladder.

Inside were other inspectors and a photographer. Three people who seemed to be reporters were looking with rather absent-minded interest at the African statues, masks, animal skins, and ostrich eggs set here and there on the walls. Entering the living room was like violating the privacy of a hunter's lair.

Two women were hunched together, sobbing. They looked very much alike, the same straight forehead, the same curved nose, the same dark circles about eyes reddened from crying. The one in the pale dress was speaking: "After my nap, I felt like taking a bath. The door was locked from the inside"—blowing her nose— "and I thought to myself, it's the maid taking her bath. I say 'the maid,'" she corrected, "but we never called her anything else but her name, Diouana. I waited for more than an hour, but didn't see her come out. I went back and called, knocking on the door. There was no answer. Then I phoned our neighbor, the Commodore. . ."

She stopped, wiped her nose, and began to cry again. Her sister, the younger of the two, hair cut in a boyish style, sat hanging her head.

"You're the one who discovered the body?"

"Yes. . . that is, when Madame Pouchet called and told me that the black girl had locked herself in the bathroom, I thought it was a joke. I spent thirty-five years at sea, you know. I've roamed the seven seas. I'm retired from the Navy."

"Yes, yes, we know."

"Yes, well, when Madame Pouchet called I brought my ladder."

"You brought the ladder?"

"No. It was Mademoiselle Dubois, Madame's sister,

who suggested the idea. And when I got to the window, I saw the black girl swimming in blood."

"Where is the key to the door?"

"Here it is, your Honor," said the inspector.

"Just wanted to see it."

"I've checked the window," said the other inspector.

"I'm the one who opened it, after breaking the pane," said the retired navy man.

"Which pane did you break?"

"Which pane?" he repeated. He was wearing white linen trousers and a blue jacket.

"Yes, I saw it, but I'd like to ask precisely."

"The second from the top," answered the sister.

At this, two stretcher-bearers came down, carrying a body wrapped in a blanket. Blood dripped on the steps. The magistrate lifted a corner of the blanket and frowned. A black girl lay dead on the stretcher, her throat cut from one ear to the other.

"It was with this knife. A kitchen knife," said another man, from the top of the stairs.

"Did you bring her from Africa or did you hire her here?"

"We brought her back from Africa, in April. She came by boat. My husband is with aerial navigation in Dakar, but the company only pays air passage for the family. She worked for us in Dakar. For two and a half or three years."

"How old was she?"

"I don't know exactly."

"According to her passport, she was born in 1927."

"Oh! The natives don't know when they are born," offered the naval officer, plunging his hands in his pockets.

"I don't know why she killed herself. She was well treated here, she ate the same food, shared the same rooms as my children."

"And your husband, where is he?"

"He left for Paris the day before yesterday."

"Ah!" said the inspector, still looking at the knick-knacks. "Why do you think it was suicide?"

"Why?" said the retired officer. . . "Oh! Who do you think would make an attempt on the life of a Negro girl? She never went out. She didn't know anyone, except for Madame's children."

The reporters were getting impatient. The suicide of a maid—even if she were black—didn't amount to a hill of beans. There was nothing newsworthy in it.

"It must have been homesickness. Because lately, she'd been behaving very strangely. She wasn't the same."

The police magistrate went upstairs, accompanied by one of the inspectors. They examined the bathroom, the window.

"Some boomerang, this story," said the inspector.

The others waited in the living room.

"We'll let you know when the coroner is finished," said the inspector, on his way out with the police magistrate an hour after their arrival.

The cars and the reporters left. In the Villa of Green Happiness the two women and the retired naval officer remained silent.

Bit by bit, Madame Pouchet searched her memory. She thought back to Africa and her elegant villa on the road to Hann. She remembered Diouana pushing open the iron gate and signaling to the German shepherd to stop barking.

It was there, in Africa, that everything had started. Diouana had made the six-kilometer round trip on foot three times a week. For the last month she had made it gaily, enraptured, her heart beating as if she were in love for the first time. Beginning at the outskirts of Dakar, brand-new houses were scattered like jewels in a landscape of cactus, bougainvillea and jasmine. The asphalt of the Avenue Gambetta stretched out like a long black ribbon. Joyous and happy as usual, the little maid had no complaints about the road or her employers.

Though it was a long way, it had no longer seemed so for the past month, ever since Madame had announced she would take her to France. France! Diouana shouted the word in her head. Everything around her had become ugly, the magnificent villas she had so often admired seemed shabby.

In order to be able to travel, in order to go to France, since she was originally from the Casamance, she had needed an identity card. All her paltry savings went to get one. "So what?" she thought. "I'm on my way to France!"

"Is that you, Diouana?"

"Viye, Madame," came her answer in the Senegalese accent. She spoke from the vestibule, nicely dressed in her light colored cotton, her hair neatly combed.

"Good! Monsieur is in town. Will you look after the children?"

"Viye, Madame," she agreed in her childish voice.

Though her identity card read "born in 1927," Diouana was not yet thirty. But she must have been over twenty-one. She went to find the children. Every room was in the same condition. Parcels packed and tied with strings, boxes piled here and there. After ten whole days of washing and ironing, there wasn't much left for Diouana to do. In the proper sense of her duties, she was a laundress. There was a cook, a houseboy and herself. Three people. The servants.

"Diouana. . . Diouana," Madame called.

"Madame?" she answered, emerging from the children's room.

Madame was standing with a notebook in her hands making an inventory of the baggage. The movers would be coming at any moment.

"Have you been to see your parents? Do you think they will be happy?"

"Viye, Madame. The whole family is agreed. I tell Mama for myself. Also tell Papa Boutoupa," she said.

Her face, which had been radiant with happiness, fixed on the empty walls, and began to fade. Her heartbeat slowed. She would be ill if Madame changed her mind. Ready to plead her case, Diouana's ebony-black face grew gloomy, she lowered her eyes.

"You're not going to tell me at the last moment, on this very day, that you're leaving us in the lurch?"

"No, Madame, me go."

They were not speaking the same language. Diouana wanted to see France, this country whose beauty, richness, and joy of living everyone praised. She wanted to see it and make a triumphal return. This was where people got rich. Already, without having left African soil, she could see herself on the dock, returning from France, wealthy to the millions, with gifts of clothes for everyone. She dreamed of the freedom to go where she wished, without having to work like a beast of burden. If Madame should change her mind, refuse to take her, it would truly make her ill.

As for Madame, she was remembering the last few holidays she had spent in France. Three of them. And then she had only had two children. In Africa, Madame had acquired bad habits when it came to servants. In France when she hired a maid not only was the salary higher, but the maid demanded a day off to boot. Madame had had to let her go and hired another. The next one was no different from the first, if not worse. She answered Madame tit for tat. "Anyone who is capable of having children should take a turn with them herself. I can't live in. I have my own children to take care of and a husband too," she declared.

Used to being waited on hand and foot, Madame had yielded to her wifely duties, and clumsily fulfilled the role of mother. As for a real vacation, she had hardly had any. She soon persuaded her husband to return to Africa.

On her return, grown thin and thoroughly exasperated, she had conceived a plan for her next vacation. She put want ads in all the newspapers. A hundred young girls answered. Her choice fell on Diouana, newly arrived from her native bush. Producing two more children during the three years that Diouana worked for her, between her last holiday and the one to come, Madame sang the praises of France. For three thousands francs a month, any young African girl would have followed her to the end of the earth. And to top it off, from time to time, especially lately, Madame would give Diouana little gifts of this and that, old clothes, shoes that could be mended.

This was the insurmountable moat that separated the maid and her employer.

"Did you give Monsieur your identity card?"

"Viye, Madame."

"You may go back to your work. Tell the cook to give the three of you a good meal."

"Merci, Madame," she answered, and went off to the kitchen.

Madame continued her inventory.

Monsieur returned on the stroke of noon, his arrival announced by the barking of the dog. Getting out of his Peugeot 403, he found his wife, indefatigable, pencil in hand.

"Haven't the baggage men come yet?" she said nervously.

"They'll be here at a quarter to two. Our bags will be on top. That way they'll be out first when we land in Marseille. And what about Diouana? Diouana!"

The eldest of the children ran to fetch her. She was under the trees with the littlest one.

"Viye, Madame."

"It's Monsieur who was calling you."

"That's fine. Here are your ticket and your identity card."

Diouana held out a hand to take them.

"You keep the identity card, I'll take care of the

ticket. The Duponts are returning on the same ship, they'll look after you. Are you glad to be going to France?"

"Viye, Monsieur."

"Good. Where are your bags?"

"At Rue Escarfait, Monsieur."

"After I've had lunch we'll go fetch them in the car."

"Bring the children in, Diouana, it's time for their nap."

"Viye, Madame."

Diouana wasn't hungry. The cook's helper, two years younger than she, brought the plates and took the empty ones away, noiselessly. The cook was sweating heavily. He wasn't happy. He was going to be out of work. This was how the departure affected him. And for this reason he was a bit resentful of the maid. Leaning out the wide window overlooking the sea, transported, Diouana watched the birds flying high above in the immense expanse of blue. In the distance she could barely make out the Island of Gorée. She was holding her identity card, turning it over and over, examining it and smiling quietly to herself. The picture was a gloomy one. She wasn't pleased with the pose or with the exposure. "What does it matter? I'm leaving!", she thought.

"Samba," said Monsieur, who had come to the kitchen, "the meal was excellent today. You outdid yourself. Madame is very pleased with you."

The cook's helper stood at attention. Samba, the cook, adjusted his tall white hat and made an effort to smile.

"Thank you very much, Monsieur," he said. "I too am happy, very happy, because Monsieur and Madame are happy. Monsieur very nice. My family big, unhappy. Monsieur leave, me no more work."

"We'll be back, my good man. And then, with your talent you'll soon find another job!"

Samba, the cook, wasn't so sure. The Whites were stingy. And in a Dakar filled with country people each claiming to be a master cook, it wouldn't be easy to find a job.

"We'll be back, Samba. Maybe sooner than you think. The last time we stayed only two and half months."

To these consoling words from Madame, who had joined her husband in the kitchen, Samba could only answer: "Merci, Madame. Madame very nice lady."

Madame was glad. She knew from experience what it meant to have a good reputation with the servants.

"You can go home this afternoon at four with Monsieur. I'll pack up the rest. When we come back I promise to hire you again. Are you pleased?"

"Merci, Madame."

Madame and Monsieur were gone. Samba gave Diouana a slap. She hit him back angrily.

"Hey! Careful. Careful. You're going away today. So we shouldn't fight."

"That hurt!" she said.

"And Monsieur, does he hurt you too?"

Samba suspected a secret liaison between the maid and her employer.

"They're calling for you, Diouana. I hear the car starting."

She left without even saying goodbye.

The car moved along the highway. Diouana didn't often have the privilege of being driven by Monsieur. Her very look invited the pedestrians' admiration, though she dared not wave a hand or shout while going past, "I'm on my way to France!" Yes, France! She was sure her happiness was plain to see. The subterranean sources of this tumultuous joy made her a bit shaky. When the car stopped in front of the house at Rue Escarfait, she was surprised. "Already?" she thought. Next door to her humble house, at the Gay Navigator Café a few customers were seated at the tables and several were talking quietly on the sidewalk.

"Is it today you're leaving, little one?" asked Tive

Correa. Already tipsy, he steadied himself, legs apart, holding his bottle by the neck. His clothes were rumpled.

Diouana would have nothing to do with the drunkard. She didn't listen to Tive Correa's advice. An old sailor, Tive Correa had come home from Europe after twenty years absence. He had left, rich with youth, full of ambition, and come home a wreck. From having wanted everything he had returned with nothing but an excessive love for the bottle. For Diouana he predicted nothing but misfortune. Once, when she had asked his advice, his opinion had been that she shouldn't go. In spite of his serious state of inebriety, he made a few steps towards Monsieur, bottle still in hand.

"Is it true that Diouana's leaving with you Monsieur?"

Monsieur did not answer. He took out a cigarette and lit it, blew the smoke through the car door, and looked Tive Correa over from head to toe. What a bum he was, greasy clothes, stinking of palm wine. Correa leaned over, putting a hand on the car door.

"I was there. I lived in France for twenty years," he began, with a note of pride in his voice. "I, whom you see this way, ruin though I am today, I know France better than you do. During the war I lived in Toulon, and the Germans sent us with the other Africans to Aix-en-Provence, to the mines at Gardanne. I've been against her going."

"We haven't forced her to go! She wants to." Monsieur answered dryly.

"Certainly. What young African doesn't dream of going to France? Unfortunately, they confuse living in France with being a servant in France. I come from the village next to Diouana's, in Casamance. There, we don't say the way you do that it is the light that attracts the butterfly, but the other way round. In my country, Casamance, we say that the darkness pursues the butterfly."

In the meantime, Diouana returned, escorted by several

women. They were chatting along, each begging for a
little souvenir. Diouana promised happily; she was smiling, her white teeth gleaming.

"The others are at the dock," said one. "Don't forget
my dress."

"For me, some shoes for the children. You've got the
size in your suitcase. And remember the sewing machine."

"The petticoats, too."

"Write and tell me how much the hair straightening
irons cost and also the price of a red jacket with big
buttons, size 44."

"Don't forget to send a little money to your mother
in Boutoupa. . ."

Each one had something to tell her, some request to
make of her; Diouana promised. Her face was radiant.
Tive Correa took the suitcase, pushing it drunkenly but
not roughly into the car.

"Let her go, girls. Do you think money grows on trees
in France? She'll have something to say about that when
she gets back."

Loud protests from the women.

"Goodbye, little cousin. Take care of yourself. You have
the address of the cousin in Toulon. Write to him as
soon as you get there, he will help you. Come give me a
kiss."

They all kissed each other goodbye. Monsieur was
getting impatient. He started up the motor to indicate
politely that he wished they'd be done with it.

The Peugeot was moving. Everyone waved.

At the dock it was the same; relatives, friends, little
commissions. Everyone pressed around her. Always under
the watchful eye of Monsieur. She embarked.

A week at sea. "No news," she would have written
if she'd been keeping a diary, in which case she'd also
have had to know how to read and write. Water in
front, behind, to port, to starboard. Nothing but a sheet
of liquid, and above it, the sky.

When the boat landed, Monsieur was there. After the formalities, they quickly made their way to the Côte d'Azur. She devoured everything with her eyes, marvelling, astonished. She packed every detail into her head. It was beautiful. Africa seemed a sordid slum by comparison. Towns, buses, trains, trucks went by along the coastal highway. The heaviness of the traffic surprised her.

"Did you have a good crossing?"

"Viye, Monsieur," she would have answered, if Monsieur had asked the question.

After a two-hour drive, they were in Antibes.

Days, weeks and the first month went by. The third began. Diouana was no longer the joyous young girl with the ready laugh, full of life. Her eyes were beginning to look hollow, her glance was less alert, she no longer noticed details. She had a lot more work to do here than in Africa. At first her fretting was hardly noticeable. Of France, "La Belle France," she had only a vague idea, a fleeting vision. French gardens, the hedges of the other villas, the crests of roofs appearing above the green trees, the palms. Everyone lived his own life, isolated, shut up in his own house. Monsieur and Madame went out a good deal, leaving her with the four children. The children quickly organized a mafia and persecuted her. "You've got to keep them happy," Madame would say. The oldest, a real scamp, recruited others of like inclination and they played explorer. Diouana was the "savage." The children pestered her. Once in a while the eldest got a good spanking. Having picked up phrases from the conversations of mama, papa or the neighbors back in Africa—phrases in which notions of racial prejudice played a part—he made exaggerated remarks to his pals. Without the knowledge of his parents, they would turn up, chanting, "Black Girl, Black Girl. She's as black as midnight."

Perpetually harassed, Diouana began to waste away. In Dakar she had never had to think about the color of her skin. With the youngsters teasing she began to question it. She understood that here she was alone. There was nothing that connected her with the others. And it aggravated her, poisoned her life, the very air she breathed.

Everything grew blunt; her old dreams, her contentment eroded. She did a lot of hard work. It was she who did all the cooking, laundry, babysitting, ironing. Madame's sister came to stay at the villa, making seven people to look after. At night, as soon as she went up to bed, Diouana slept like a log.

The venom was poisoning her heart. She had never hated anything. Everything became monotonous. Where was France? The beautiful cities she had seen at the movies in Dakar, the rare foods, the interesting crowds? The population of France reduced itself to these spiteful monsters, Monsieur, Madame and Mademoiselle, who had become strangers to her. The country seemed limited to the immediate surroundings of the villa. Little by little she was drowning. The wide horizons of a short while ago stopped now at the color of her skin, which suddenly filled her with an invincible terror. Her skin. Her blackness. Timidly, she retreated into herself.

With no one from her universe to exchange ideas with, she held long moments of palaver with herself. A week ago, Monsieur and Madame had cleverly taken her along to visit their relatives in Cannes.

"Tomorrow we'll go to Cannes. My parents have never tasted African food. You'll do us Africans honor with your cooking," Madame had said. She was nearly bare, and getting bronzed from the sun.

"Viye, Madame."

"I've ordered some rice and two chickens. . . You'll be careful not to spice it too much?"

"Viye, Madame."

Answering this way, her heart hardened. It seemed the hundredth time that she'd been trailed from villa to villa. To this one's house and then to that one's. It was at the Commodore's—everyone called him the Commodore—that she had rebelled the first time. Some silly people, who followed her about, hanging on her heels in the kitchen, had been there for dinner. Their presence was an oppressive shadow on her slightest movement. She had the feeling of not knowing how to do anything. These strange, self-centered, sophisticated beings never stopped asking her idiotic questions about how African women do their cooking. She kept herself under control.

The three women were still chirping when she waited on them at the table, testing the first spoonful on the tip of their tongues, then gluttonously devouring the rest.

"This time, at my parents, you must outdo yourself."

"Viye, Madame."

Restored to her kitchen, her thoughts went to Madame's former kindness. She detested it. Madame had been good to her, but in a self-seeking way. The only reason for her attentiveness had been to wind the strings round Diouana, the better to make her sweat. She loathed everything. Back in Dakar, Diouana used to gather Monsieur and Madame's leftovers to take home to Rue Escarfait. She had taken pride then in working for "important white people." Now she was so alone their meals made her sick to her stomach. The resentment spoiled her relations with her employers. She stood her ground, they stood theirs. They no longer exchanged any remarks but those of a business nature.

"Diouana, will you do the washing today?"

"Viye, Madame."

"Last time you didn't to a good job on my slips. The iron was too hot. And the collars on Monsieur's shirt were scorched. Do pay attention to what you're doing, will you?"

"Viye, Madame."

"Oh, I forgot. There are some buttons missing on Monsieur's shirts and his shorts."

Every little job was Diouana's. And then Madame started speaking to her in pidgin French, even in front of guests. And this was the only thing she did with honesty. In the end, no one in the house ever spoke to the maid any more except in terms of "Missie," Senegalese pidgin talk. Bewildered by her inadequacies in French, Diouana closed herself into a sort of solitary confinement. After long, lonely moments of meditation she came to the conclusion first of all that she was nothing but a useful object, and furthermore that she was being put on exhibit like a trophy. At parties, when Monsieur or Madame made remarks about "native" psychology, Diouana was taken as an illustration. The neighbors would say: "It's the Pouchets' black girl. . ." She wasn't "the African girl" in her own right, but theirs. And that hurt.

The fourth month began. Things got worse. Her thoughts grew more lucid every day. She had work and work to spare. All week long. Sunday was Mademoiselle's favorite day for asking friends over. There were lots of them. The weeks began and ended with them.

Everything became clear. Why had Madame wanted her to come? Her generosities had been premeditated. Madame no longer took care of her children. She kissed them every morning, that was all. And where was "La Belle France?" These questions kept repeating themselves. "I am cook, nursemaid, chambermaid; I do all the washing and ironing and for a mere three thousand francs a month. I do housework for six people. What am I doing here?"

Diouana gave way to her memories. She compared her "native bush" to these dead shrubs. How different from the forest of her home in Casamance. The memory of her village, of the community life, cut her off from the others even more. She bit her lips, sorry to have come. And on this film of the past, a thousand other details were projected.

Returning to these surroundings, where she was doubly an outsider, her feelings hardened. She thought often of Tive Correa. His predictions had come cruelly true. She would have liked to write to him, but couldn't. Since arriving in France, she had had only two letters from her mother. She didn't have the time to answer, even though Madame had promised to write for her. Was it possible to tell Madame what she was thinking? She was angry with herself. Her ignorance made her mute. It was infuriating. And besides, Mademoiselle had made off with her stamps.

A pleasant idea crossed her mind though, and raised a smile. This evening only Monsieur was at home, watching television. She decided to take advantage of the opportunity. Then, unexpectedly finding Madame there too, Diouana stopped abruptly and left the room.

"Sold, sold. Bought, bought," she repeated to herself. "They've bought me. For three thousand francs I do all this work. They lured me, tied me to them, and I'm stuck here like a slave." She was determined now. That night she opened her suitcase, looked at the objects in it and wept. No one cared.

Yet she went through the same motions and remained as sealed off from the others as an oyster at low tide on the beach of her native Casamance.

"Douna"—it was Mademoiselle calling her. Why was it impossible for her to say Di-ou-a-na?

Her anger redoubled. Mademoiselle was even lazier than Madame: "Come take this away"—"There is such-and-such to be done, Douna"—"Why don't you do this, Douna?"—"Douna, now and then please rake the garden." For an answer Mademoiselle would receive an incendiary glance. Madame complained about her to Monsieur.

"What is the matter with you, Diouana? Are you ill or something?" he asked.

She no longer opened her mouth.

"You can tell me what's the matter. Perhaps you'd like to go to Toulon. I haven't had the time to go, but tomorrow I'll take you with me."

"Anyone would think we disgust her," said Madame.

Three days later Diouana took her bath. Returning home after a morning of shopping, Madame Pouchet went in the bathroom and quickly emerged.

"Diouana! Diouana!" she called. "You *are* dirty, in spite of everything. You might have left the bathroom clean."

"No me, Madame. It was the children, viye."

"The children! The children are tidy. It may be that you're fed up with them. But to find you telling lies, like a native, *that* I don't like. I don't like liars and you are a liar!"

Diouana kept silent, though her lips were trembling. She went upstairs to the bathroom, and took her clothes off. It was there they found her, dead.

"Suicide," the investigators concluded. The case was closed.

The next day, in the newspaper on page four, column six, hardly noticeable, was a small headline:

"Homesick African Girl Cuts Throat in Antibes."

THE TRULY MARRIED WOMAN

Abioseh Nicol

Born in Sierra Leone, Abioseh Nicol received his
education in that country, Nigeria, and England.
Although he studied medicine at the Universities of
London and Cambridge, Dr. Nicol has long been
known throughout African literary circles as a crafts-
man of the short story. He has published numerous
articles and short stories in African, English, and
American publications; and in 1952 was awarded
the Margaret Wrong Prize and Medal for Literature in Africa. "The Truly Married Woman" is
from his collection, *The Truly Married Woman and
Other Stories* (1965).

I

AJAYI stirred for a while and then sat up. He looked at
the cheap alarm clock on the chair by his bedside. It
was six-fifteen, and light outside already; the African
town was slowly waking to life. The night watchmen
roused from sleep by the angry crowing of cockerels
were officiously banging the locks of stores and houses to
assure themselves and their employers, if near, of their
efficiency. Village women were tramping through the
streets to the market place with their wares, arguing
and gossiping.

Ajayi sipped his cup of morning tea. It was as he liked
it, weak and sugary, without milk. With an effort of
will, he got up and walked to the window, and standing there he took six deep breaths. This done daily, he

firmly believed, would prevent tuberculosis. He walked through his ramshackle compound to an outhouse and took a quick bath, pouring the water over his head from a tin cup with which he scooped water from a bucket.

By then Ayo had laid out his breakfast. Ayo was his wife. Not really one, he would explain to close friends, but a mistress. A good one. She had borne him three children and was now three months gone with another. They had been together for twelve years. She was a patient, handsome woman. Very dark with very white teeth and open sincere eyes. Her hair was always carefully plaited. When she first came to him—to the exasperation of her parents—he had fully intended marrying her as soon as she had shown satisfactory evidence of fertility, but he had never quite got round to it. In the first year or so she would report to him in great detail the splendor of the marriage celebrations of her friends, looking at him with hopeful eyes. He would close the matter with a tirade on the sinfulness of ostentation. She gave up after some time. Her father never spoke to her again after she had left home. Her mother visited her secretly and attended the baptismal ceremonies of all her children. The Church charged etxra for illegitimate children as a deterrent; two dollars instead of fifty cents. Apart from this, there was no other great objection. Occasionally, two or three times a year, the pastor would preach violently against adultery, polygamy, and unmarried couples living together. Ajayi and Ayo were good church-people and attended regularly, but sat in different pews. After such occasions, their friends would sympathize with them and other couples in similar positions. There would be a little grumbling and the male members of the congregation would say that the trouble with the Church was that it did not stick to its business of preaching the Gospel, but meddled in people's private lives. Ajayi would indignantly absent himself from Church for a few weeks but would go back eventually because he liked

singing hymns and because he knew secretly that the
pastor was right.

Ayo was a good mistress. Her father was convinced
she could have married a high-school teacher at least,
or a pharmacist, but instead she had attached herself to a
junior Government clerk. But Ayo loved Ajayi, and was
happy in her own slow, private way. She cooked his
meals and bore him children. In what spare time she
had she either did a little petty trading, visited friends,
or gossiped with Omo, the woman next door.

With his towel round his waist, Ajayi strode back to
the bedroom, dried himself and dressed quickly but
carefully in his pink tussore suit. He got down the new
bottle of patent medicine which one of his friends who
worked in a drug store had recommended to him. Ajayi
believed that to keep healthy, a man must regularly take
a dose of some medicine. He read the label of this one.
It listed about twenty diseased conditions of widely
differing pathology which the contents of the bottle
were reputed to cure if the patient persevered in its daily
intake. Ajayi underlined in his own mind at least six
from which he believed he either suffered or was on the
threshold of suffering: dizziness, muscle pain, impotence,
fever, jaundice, and paralytic tremors. Intelligence and
courage caused him to skip the obviously female maladies
and others such as nervous debility or bladder pains. It
said on the label too that a teaspoonful should be taken
three times a day. But since he only remembered to take
it in the morning and in any case believed in stock treatment, he took a swig and two large gulps. The medicine
was bitter and astringent. He grimaced but was satisfied.
It was obviously a good and strong medicine or else it
would not have been so bitter.

He went in to breakfast. He soon finished his maize
porridge, fried beans, and cocoa. He then severely flogged
his eldest son, a ten-year-old boy, for wetting his sleeping-

mat last night. Ayo came in after the boy had fled screaming to the back yard.

"Ajayi, you flog that boy too much," she said. "He
should stop wetting the floor, he is a big boy," he replied.
"In any case, no one is going to instruct me on how to
bring up my son." "He is mine too," Ayo said. She seldom
opposed him unless she felt strongly about something.
"He has not stopped wetting although you beat him every
time he does. In fact, he is doing it more and more
now. Perhaps if you stopped whipping him he might get
better." "Did I whip him to begin doing it?" Ajayi
asked. "No." "Well, how will stopping whipping him
stop him doing it?" Ajayi asked triumphantly. "Neverthe-
less," Ayo said, "our own countrywoman Bimbola, who
has just come back from England and America studying
nursing, told us in a women's group meeting that it
was wrong to punish children for such things." "All
right, I'll see," he said, reaching for his sun helmet.

All that day at the office he thought about this and
other matters. So Ayo had been attending women's
meetings. Well, what do you know. She would be running
for the Town Council next. The sly woman. Always looking so quiet and meek and then quoting modern theories
from overseas doctors at him. He smiled with pride. Indeed Ayo was an asset. Perhaps it was wrong to beat the
boy. He decided he would not do so again.

Towards closing time the chief clerk sent for him. Wondering what mistake he had made that day, or on what
mission he was to be sent, he hurried along to the forward office. There were three white men sitting on chairs
by the chief clerk, who was an ageing African dressed with
severe respectability. On seeing them, Ajayi's heart started
thudding. The police, he thought; heavens, what have
I done?

"Mr. Ajayi, these gentlemen have enquired for you,"
the chief clerk said formally. "Pleased to meet you, Mr.
Ajayi," the tallest said, with a smile. "We represent the

World Gospel Crusading Alliance from Minnesota. My name is Jonathan Olsen." Ajayi shook hands and the other two were introduced.

"You expressed an interest in our work a year ago and we have not forgotten. We are on our way to India and we thought we would look you up personally."

It transpired that the three Crusaders were en route and that their ship had stopped for refueling off the Africa port for a few hours. The chief clerk looked at Ajayi with new respect. Ajayi tried desperately to remember any connection with W.G.C.A. (as Olsen by then had proceeded to call it) whilst he made conversation with them a little haltingly. Then suddenly he remembered. Some time ago he had got hold of a magazine from his subtenant who worked at the United States Information Service. He had cut a coupon from it and posted it to W.G.C.A. asking for information, but really hoping that they would send illustrated Bibles free which he might give away or sell. He hoped for at least large reproductions of religious paintings which, suitably framed, would decorate his parlor or which he might paste up on his bedroom wall. But nothing had come of it and he had forgotten. Now here was W.G.C.A. as large as life. Three lives. Instantly and recklessly he invited all three and the chief clerk to come to his house for a cold drink. They all agreed.

"Mine is a humble abode," he warned them. "No abode is humble that is illumined by Christian love," Olsen replied. "His is illumined all right, I can assure you," the chief clerk remarked drily.

Olsen suggested a taxi, but Ajayi neatly blocked that by saying the roads were bad. He had hurriedly whispered to a fellow clerk to rush home on a bicycle and tell Ayo he was coming in half an hour with white men and that she should clean up and get fruit drinks. Ayo was puzzled by the message as she firmly imagined all white men drank only whisky and iced beer. But the messenger had

said that there was a mixture of friendliness and piety
in the visitors' mien, which made him suspect that they
might be missionaries. Another confirmatory point was
that they were walking instead of being in a car. That
cleared up the anomaly in Ayo's mind and she set to
work at once. Oju, now recovered from his morning
disgrace, was dispatched with a basket on his head to
buy soft drinks. Ayo whisked off the wall all their commercial calendars with suggestive pictures. She propped
up family photographs which had fallen face downwards
on the table. She removed the Wild West novels and
romance magazines from the parlour and put instead an
old copy of Bunyan's *Pilgrim's Progress* and a prayer book
which she believed would add culture and religious force
to the decorations. She remembered the wine glasses
and the beer-advertising table-mats in time and put those
under the sofa. She just had time to change to her Sunday frock and borrow a wedding ring from her neighbor
when Ajayi and the guests arrived. The chief clerk was
rather surprised at the change in the room—which he
had visited before—and in Ayo's dress and ring. But he
concealed his feelings. Ayo was introduced and made a
little conversation in English. This pleased Ajayi a great
deal. The children had been changed too into Sunday
suits, faces washed and hair brushed. Olsen was delighted
and insisted on taking photographs for the Crusade
journal. Ayo served drinks and then modestly retired,
leaving the men to discuss serious matters. Olsen by then
was talking earnestly on the imminence of Christ's
Second Coming and offering Ajayi ordination into dea-
conship.

The visit passed off well and soon the missionaries left
to catch their boat. Ajayi had been saved from holy
orders by the chief clerk's timely explanation that it was
strictly against Government regulations for civil servants
to indulge in non-official organizations. To help Ajayi
out of his quandary, he had even gone further and said

that contravention might result in a fine or imprisonment. "Talk about colonial oppression," the youngest of the missionaries had said, gloomily.

The next day Ajayi called at the chief clerk's office with a carefully wrapped bottle of beer as a present for his help generally on the occasion. They discussed happily the friendliness and interest the white men had shown.

This incident and Ayo's protest against flagellation as a specific against enuresis made Ajayi very thoughtful for a week. He decided to marry Ayo. Another consideration which added weight to the thought was the snapshot Olsen took for his magazine. In some peculiar way Ajayi felt he and Ayo should marry, as millions of Americans would see their picture—Olsen had assured him of this—as "one saved and happy African family." He announced his intention of marrying her to Ayo one evening, after a particularly good meal and a satisfactory bout of belching. Ayo at once became extremely solicitous and got up looking at him with some anxiety. Was he ill? she asked. Was there anything wrong at the office? Had anyone insulted him? No, he answered, there was nothing wrong with his wanting to get married, was there? Or had she anyone else in mind? Ayo laughed, "As you will," she said; "let us get married, but do not say I forced you into it."

They discussed the wedding that night. Ajayi wanted to have a white wedding with veil and orange blossom. But Ayo with regret decided it would not be quite right. They agreed on grey. Ayo particularly wanted a corset to strap down her obvious bulge; Ajayi gave way gallantly to this feminine whim, chucking her under the chin and saying, "You women with your vanity!" But he was firm about no honeymoon. He said he could not afford the expense and that one bed was as good as another. Ayo gave way on that. They agreed, however, on a church wedding and that their children could act as bridal pages to keep the cost of clothes within the family.

That evening Ajayi, inflamed by the idea and arrangements for the wedding, pulled Ayo excitedly to him as they lay in bed. "No," said Ayo, shyly, pushing him back gently, "you mustn't. Wait until after the marriage." "Why?" said Ajayi, rather surprised, but obedient. "Because it will not somehow be right," Ayo replied seriously and determinedly.

Ayo's father unbent somewhat when he heard of the proposed marriage. He insisted, however, that Ayo move herself and all her possessions back home to his house. The children were sent to Ayo's married sister. Most of Ajayi's family were in favor of the union, except his sister, who, moved by the threat implicit in Ayo's improved social position, advised Ajayi to see a soothsayer first. As Ayo had got wind of this through friends met at market on Saturday, she saw the soothsayer first and fixed things. When Ajayi and his sister called at night to see him, he consulted the oracles and pronounced future happiness, avoiding the sister's eye. The latter restrained herself from scratching the old man's face and accepted defeat.

The only other flaw in a felicitous situation had been Ayo's neighbor Omo, who had always on urgent occasions at short notice loaned Ayo her wedding ring. She had suddenly turned cold. Especially after Ayo had shown her the wedding presents Ajayi intended to give her. The neighbor had handled the flimsy nylon articles with a mixture of envy and rage.

"Do you mean you are going to wear these?" she had asked. "Yes," Ayo had replied simply. "But, my sister," she had protested, "you will catch cold with these. Suppose you had an accident and all those doctors lifted your clothes in hospital. They will see everything through these." "I never have accidents," Ayo answered, and added, "Ajayi says all the 'Ollywood cinema women wear these. It says so there. Look—'Trademark Hollywood.'" "These are disgraceful; they hide nothing, it is extremely fast of you to wear them," the jealous girl said, pushing them back furiously over the fence to Ayo.

"Why should I want to hide anything from my husband when we are married?" Ayo said triumphantly, moving back to her own kitchen and feeling safe in future from the patronizing way the wedding ring had always been lent her.

The arrangements had to be made swiftly, since time and the corset ribs were both against them; Ajayi's domestic routine was also sorely tried, especially his morning cup of tea which he badly missed. He borrowed heavily from a moneylender to pay the dowry and for the music, dancing, and feasting, and for dresses of the same pattern which Ayo and her female relations would wear after the ceremony on the wedding day.

The engagement took place quietly, Ajayi's uncle and other relations taking a Bible and a ring to Ayo's father and asking for her hand in marriage, the day before the wedding. They took with them two small girls carrying on their heads large hollow gourds. These contained articles like pins, farthings, fruit, kola nuts, and cloth. The articles were symbolic gifts to the bride from the bridegroom, so that she might be precluded in future marital disputes from saying, "Not a pin or a farthing has the blackguard given me since we got married."

On arrival at Ayo's father's house, the small procession passed it first as if uncertain, then returned to it. This gave warning to the occupants. Ajayi's uncle then knocked several times. Voices from within shouted back and ordered him to name himself, his ancestry, and his mission. He did this. Argument and some abuse followed on either side. After his family credentials had been seriously examined, questioned, doubted, and disparaged, Ajayi's uncle started wheedling and cajoling. This went on for about half an hour to the enjoyment and mock trepidation of Ajayi's relations. He himself had remained at home, waiting. Finally, Ayo's father opened the door.

Honor was satisfied and it was now supposed to be clearly evident to Ajayi's relations, in case it had not been before, that they were entering a family and household which was distinguished, difficult, and jealous of their distinction.

"What is your mission here?" Ayo's father then asked sternly.

Ajayi's uncle answered humbly:

"We have come to pluck a red, red rose
That in your beautiful garden grows.
Which never has been plucked before,
So lovelier than any other."

"Will you be able to nurture our lovely rose well?" another of Ayo's male relations asked?

Ajayi's family party replied:

"So well shall we nurture your rose
'Twill bring forth many others."

They were finally admitted; drinks were served and prayers offered. The gifts were accepted and others given in exchange. Conversation went on for about thirty minutes on every conceivable subject but the one at hand. All through this, Ayo and her sisters and some young female relations were kept hidden in an adjoining bedroom. Finally with some delicacy, Ajayi's uncle broached the subject after Ayo's father had given him an opening by asking what, apart from the honor of being entertained by himself and his family, did Ajayi's relations seek. They had heard, the latter replied, that in this very household there was a maiden chaste, beautiful, and obedient, known to all by the name of Ayo. This maiden they sought as wife for their kinsman Ajayi. Ayo's father opened the bedroom door and brought forth Ayo's sister. Was this the one? he asked, testing them. They examined her. No it was not this one they replied, this one was too short to be Ayo. Then a cousin was brought out.

Was this she? No, this one is too fat, the applicants said. About ten women in all were brought out. But none was the correct one. Each was too short or too fat or too fair, as the case was, to suit the description of the maiden they sought. At this point, Ajayi's uncle slapped his thigh, as if to show that his doubts were confirmed; turning to his party, he stated that it was a good thing they had insisted on seeing for themselves the bride demanded, or else the wrong woman would have been foisted on them. They agreed, nodding. All right, all right, Ayo's father had replied, there was no cause for impatience. He wanted to be sure they knew whom they wanted. Standing on guard at the bedroom door, he turned his back to the assembly, and with tears in his eyes beckoned to Ayo sitting on the bed inside. He kissed her lightly on the forehead to forgive the past years. Then he led her forth and turned fiercely to the audience. Was this then the girl they wanted, he asked them sternly?

"This *is* the very one," Ajayi's uncle replied with joy. "Hip, hip, hip, hooray," everybody shouted, encircling Ayo and waving white handkerchiefs over her head. The musicians smote their guitars instantly; someone beat an empty wine bottle rhythmically with a corkscrew; after a few preliminary trills the flutes rose high in melody; all danced round Ayo. And as she stood in the centre, a woman in her mid-thirties, her hair slightly streaked grey, undergoing a ceremony of honor she had often witnessed and long put outside her fate, remembering the classic description of chastity, obedience, and beauty, she wept with joy and the unborn child stirred within her for the first time.

The next morning she was bathed by an old and respected female member of her family and her mother helped her to dress. Her father gave her away at the marriage service at church. It was a quiet wedding with only sixty guests or so. Ajayi looked stiff in dinner jacket with buttonhole, an ensemble which he wore only on special occasions. Afterwards they went to Ayo's family home for the wedding luncheon. At the door they were met by another of Ayo's numerous elderly aunts, who held a glass of water to their lips for them to sip in turn, Ajayi being first. The guests were all gathered outside behind the couple. The aunt made a conveniently long speech until all the guests had foregathered. She warned Avo not to be too friendly with other women as they would inevitably steal her husband; that they should live peaceably and not let the sun go down on a quarrel between them. Turning to Ajayi, she told him with a twinkle in her eye that a wife could be quite as exciting as a mistress, and also not to use physical violence against their daughter, his wife.

After this they entered and the Western part of the ceremony took place. The wedding cake (which Ayo had made) was cut and speeches made. Then Ajayi departed to his own family home where other celebrations went on. Later he changed into a lounge suit and called for Ayo. There was weeping in Ayo's household as if she were setting off on a long journey. Her mother in saying goodbye, remarked between tears, that although she would not have the honor next morning of showing the world evidence of Ayo's virginity, yet in the true feminine powers of procreation none except the blind and deaf could say Ayo had lacked zeal.

They called on various relations on both sides of the family and at last they were home. Ayo seemed different in Ajayi's eyes. He had never really looked at her carefully before. Now he observed her head held erectly and gracefully through years of balancing loads on it in childhood; her statuesque neck with its three natural horizontal ridges—to him, signs of beauty; her handsome shoulders. He clasped her with a new tenderness.

The next morning, as his alarm clock went off, he stirred and reached for his morning cup of tea. It was not there. He sprang up and looked. Nothing. He listened for Ayo's footsteps outside in the kitchen. Nothing. He turned to look beside him. Ayo was there and her bare ebony back was heaving gently. She must be ill, he thought; all that excitement yesterday.

"Ayo, Ayo," he cried, "are you ill?" She turned round slowly still lying down and faced him. She tweaked her toes luxuriously under the cotton coverlet and patted her breast slowly. There was a terible calm about her. "No, Ajayi," she replied, "are you?" she asked him. "Are your legs paralyzed?" she continued. "No," he said. He was puzzled and alarmed, thinking that her mind had become unhinged under the strain.

"Ajayi, my husband," she said, "for twelve years I have got up every morning at five to make tea for you and breakfast. Now I am a truly married woman you must treat me with a little more respect. You are now a husband and not a lover. Get up and make yourself a cup of tea."

THE PARTY

James Matthews

James Matthews grew up in Cape Town, South
Africa, where he was born in 1929. He has worked
as a journalist in South Africa, including work with
Drum magazine. A collection of his short stories,
Azikwelwa, has been published in Sweden. "The
Party" is from *Quartet* (1963), edited by Richard
Rive.

The room was a large one, larger than any of the rooms
in the houses he had been in previously. He mentally
scaled it, comparing it with his own home. The two tiny
bedrooms and the dining-living room would take half of
this comfortable room, leaving space for the kitchen and
small yard. One end wall was covered with a tapestry and
paintings. Gilt-framed mirrors covered the other walls. In
one corner he nearly knocked an ivory carving from its
pedestal. The carpet underneath his feet was as soft and
lush as a municipal lawn.

Large as the room was, it could not contain the many
people crowding it and they spilled into the passage leading to other rooms off it.

He gave what he hoped was a polite smile as the woman squeezed into the small space left on the couch. He
could feel her thigh pressing against his own. He wanted

to edge his leg away but that would be too obvious so he
shifted his haunches to raise himself. She turned to him
and smiled.

"Don't get up, please. I know it's a bit of a jam but
we should be able to manage."

He shifted his body so that she would have a little
more space. "It's my fault," he said. "I'm taking up too
much room."

"It's kind of you to say that but I'm afraid it's my
fault, really," she laughed as she patted her hip, "taking
up far more than my allocated area."

He nodded his head as if to assure her that he also had
his troubles with a body that was not always what he
would like it to be and that he sympathised with her.

"Quite a crowd," she said.

"Yes," he replied.

"I wonder what has happened to the drinks? Have
you been served?"

"No."

"Hold on to my seat and I'll see what I can do about
it."

She was soon lost in the throng of bodies.

He changed his position so that his back rested against
the angle formed by the arm and back of the couch and
spread his legs so that they covered the area between his
neighbors and himself.

He looked at the many people in the room. There were
a lot of women, the women outnumbering the men, and
the women were all white. Of the men, there were only
four who were not white—himself and three others. The
other three he knew well. Of the whites, he knew not one.

He was a stranger amongst strangers and although they
spoke the same language, because of his color he felt that
he was deserted in a strange land.

He gazed round the room for his three friends and the
assurance they would give him.

He spotted one before the swelling line of bodies engulfed him. He had brief glimpses of another. A tight-packed group at the far end of the room attracted his attention. They parted to make way for a line of loud-talking, gesticulating women who wiggled their way across the room like a line of conga dancers on a cinema screen. Before the group re-formed, he saw Ron. Glass in hand, the other hand poked into the air, emphasizing a point, self-assured. Then the gap was closed and he could see only their backs.

He did not know what caused their interest but whatever it was, Ron would dominate the conversation.

He envied Ron his calm, cool manner, his ability to mix without restraining thoughts about color, to bridge the gap as if there was none at all or if there was a gap then it did not apply to him.

His envy was without malice and he hoped that with the passing of time he would also acquire that smoothness of manner and be forever rid of the unease he now felt.

The room was loud with speech. He could not separate the individual voices. The gruffer tones of the men merged with the shriller notes of the women, and above the roar, like clanging cymbals, their laughter.

Snatches of conversation came to him like so many broadcasts from different stations, their only link their degree of noise.

"Jack has done it again!" The announcement was greeted with laughter. "By now one would think that he would have more sense."

He wondered who Jack was and what he had done to cause the speaker's concern and the mirth of his listeners.

"Are you going to Margot's on Friday evening?"

"Yes, darling."

"Who will she have on show this time?"

"God alone knows! But if one is to judge from her previous dinners, it should be another genius of whose talent only Margot is aware. Are you going?"

"No, thanks. I'm not that hard up for a meal."

His misgivings returned. Was this what he was up against? How would he deal with them? In this jungle of polished manners and sharp tongues he would be defenceless—a black sacrificial lamb.

Ron had insisted that he go with them. The party was to celebrate the publication of a book, the author's third. Critics thought it important. With the first book published, he had become a supporter of the author, reading everything he wrote. When told by Ron that a meeting could be arranged, he had at first backed out, but the invitation, or rather Ron, had changed his mind.

"Look, William, I went to all the trouble to get you an invitation to the party so that you can meet Colin Ashworth. It's about time you started meeting people and going places," Ron had said.

He bushed when he thought of the meeting, fifteen minutes earlier.

"Colin. This is William Apollos. He swears by you as a writer," Ron said, introducing him.

He stiffly poked out a hand to meet that of a white man a head taller than himself. "How do you do?" he said, hating himself for uttering the conventional inanity.

"So this is the William you've told me about." Turning to him the white man continued, "I hear you also write, William. Would you let me have a look at some of your stuff, soon?"

He looked into a pair of understanding eyes. A choking heat filled him. "Yes . . . yes," he stammered.

"Excuse me for a moment." Their host left them to greet a couple entering.

As they crossed the room, Ron called greetings to several people, stopping to speak to some of them before passing on. During their progress William got separated from the others and had made for the couch.

A tray was being held in front of him and he smiled at the attractive red-haired woman as he reached for a glass filled with sherry. They were all so sleek and polished, yet so remote behind the party smiles. The woman sedately moved towards the next person on the couch. He looked back at the chattering throng, at the women in their form-fitting dresses with low necklines, and again he had the feeling that they should have been on a cinema screen. From where he sat, their movements gave them a three-dimensional effect, with their chatter providing the score for the scene.

Immersed in the idea, he forgot the people seated next to him and concentrated on the changing pattern. His eyes focused on a particular person, losing him then finding him again. A woman attracted his attention. She was not young but she had a bearing which compensated for her past youth. She could only play the part of a duchess or a queen. The game delighted him and he followed it in earnest, counting how many times he could pick her out before finally losing her.

He was aware that someone was looking at him and he guiltily raised his head like a little boy caught peeping at forbidden things. It was the woman who had offered to get him a drink. She had a tray on which was balanced a plate filled with snacks. There was also a bowl of mixed nuts and two glasses of gin and lime.

He jumped to his feet.

"Please, sit down," she said after seating herself, shifting her body so that he could fit himself in. He sank down beside her.

"I've brought something to nibble at. I don't think you've had anything to eat since you came. I see you've a drink at last. Oh well! You can have this one too."

"No, thank you."

"Do have it," she urged him. "Besides, I've been here longer than you."

He took the second drink, carefully placing his empty glass at the side of the tray.

"What do you do?" The friendliness of her smile soothed his wariness.

"I write," he said, "at least, I try."

"Have you had anything published?"

"Five." Then he stopped, dismayed at the schoolboy eagerness shown.

"Where were they published?" she prompted.

"They were all published locally, except for one—'The Flower Seller'—which was published in London."

"Wait a minute! I think I've read it. Yes, I have. It was in *Argosy*, wasn't it? I loved it. So you're William Apollos." A glow of warmth swept over him at her remembering the name of the writer. "You also wrote 'The Char's Birthday Wish' and 'The Golden Penny'. I always thought those stories were not written by a white writer. They were too authentic, too close to the subject." She touched him lightly on the shoulder. "You know what I mean. I must say it's a pleasure meeting you after enjoying your stories so much."

She held out her hand. "I'm Margot Pearce." He gingerly wrapped his hand around her soft one. He wondered whether she was the same Margot who invited the dullest people to her dinners. As if to confirm it, she said, "You must come to dinner and a drink at my place, then we could really have a talk. There are some people I would like you to meet." She mentioned a few names—writers, artists, a sculptor—people Ron had told him about. Not too well-known names but all considered as going to make their mark.

He burst out laughing. He could not help it as he thought of the two women and their conversation. How wrong both of them must be. If the people she mentioned were dull then the company those two moved in must be the wittiest and the most talented in the land.

She looked at him, puzzled. "Is it so funny, my asking you to dinner?"

"No, it's not that. I just thought of something someone else had said." At the same time telling himself that it had its funny side. Dinner in a big house, he imagined it would be, at a long table covered with a stiffly starched white cloth on which would be placed an array of knives and forks. At home, his mother always served dinner in the kitchen. The only time they ate in the dinning room was on religious holidays.

"When would you be able to come? Would next Friday do? I could arrange for someone to pick you up or, if you prefer, you could come out by bus. I'm at Three Anchor Bay—St. John's Road. You can't miss it. In a small house with a block of flats on each side."

He searched for an excuse. There is a difference between a party like this and a dinner. Here, there was the safety of numbers. He could withdraw himself into himself and be lost in the shuffle, but a dinner party would be more intimate. Would he know the right thing to do? What if he should choose the wrong spoon or fork? Would they laugh at his blunder or would they ignore it and try to cover it with their talk? Both ways would be painful to him. It would be better to refuse.

He was undecided. He very much wanted to be in the company of the people she had mentioned. He felt the need to mix with those who had the same yearnings as himself. From across the room Ron waved at him before being swept up into another group. He felt reassured. He would go.

"I would be less bother if I came out by bus."

"It's no bother, William."

"I'm sure I would be able to find the place on my own, ma'am."

"I shall be very angry if you don't call me Margot. Everyone else does."

He rolled her name on his tongue a few times, savoring it before uttering: "Margot."

"Margot, dear! I don't think I've been introduced to your friend."

He looked up at a tall, slender, young man—a study in black and white. Dark hair brushed flat on the skull contrasting sharply with the pale face. His eyes matched his hair and above them his eyebrows were two streaks of black. He was dressed in a black suit and pencil-slim black tie.

"Oh. It's you, Edward. Meet William Apollos. He's going to be a first-rate writer. Remember, I'm the one who told you!" She turned towards him. "William, this is Edward Blakely."

Both name and face were familiar. Then he recalled both. Blakely was a member of the Liberal Party or the Congress of Democrats, he wasn't sure which. Again he felt that awkwardness when he shook hands.

"William is coming to dinner next Friday. You're still coming, aren't you?"

"Of course, Margot." Then to William. "Would you excuse us for a moment? There're some people who want to meet Margot."

"Not at all." He felt bold enough to add, "Then I'll see you next Friday, Margot."

"Yes, and do bring along some of your work."

He leaned back breathing deeply. The bustling scene, was he to be part of it? Would he be able to fit in freely without the constant inner fear that perhaps he did not belong?

The thought which had plagued him returned. Would she have asked him to dinner if he had not been the writer of the stories she had enjoyed so much? What would her reactions have been if he had told her otherwise? That he was as nondescript as he looked, that he had come mainly because of Ron's urgings?

The doubt resurrected other doubts he had tried to bury. These people, Ron had said, made no fuss about the color of one's skin; they accepted one for what one was. Were they really so open and casual or was it a pose they all assumed?

"Do you intend sitting on this couch for the rest of the evening?" Ron stood in front of him. "What's happened to Margot? I saw her speaking to you a little while ago."

"She left with another chap, Edward Blakely, who said there were some people who wanted to meet her."

"Oh, Edward. Looking like a corpse as usual with his pale face and black eyes. What do you think of Margot?"

"She seems to be quite nice. She's . . ."

"Yes, I know. She's invited you to dinner. She fancies herself as a patron of the arts. She should have lived in the eighteenth century—then she could have turned her home into a *salon*. At least you are making progress. It's about time you crawled out of your shell. It's at parties like this that you meet people, important people, who can help you a lot if you go about it the right way."

He made no reply, silently wondering what was the right way.

Recalling Ron's attitude nine months ago, he was not sure whether he should be grateful now. He had had his first story published. Previously, Ron had scarcely spoken a dozen words to him, including him amongst those he tolerated but never asked to meet the white friends of whom he spoke so intimately and whose names so often featured in the social pages of the local newspapers. The few times Ron had spoken to him, he had repeatedly pointed out William's lack of feeling for art in any form.

His story had brought a change.

"I've read your story," Ron had said. "It's not a bad effort. Is it your first?"

"No, it's not," he replied. "I've written several, but this is the first one published."

"Why all the secrecy? Why didn't you tell me you're interested in creative writing? There are some chaps I could have introduced you to. Established writers."

A second and a third story published made him a member of the select few Ron favored.

"Come along with us, tomorrow evening. Tom Hopkirk is having a party at his place on Devil's Peak."

"No," he had replied.

Over the months, Ron had often urged him to accom-

pany them but always his answer was "No." The picture
of himself mixing socially with whites filled him with
dread. The whites at work smiled with him and spoke to
him, then forgot him, remembering him only when they
wanted something done. But the more Ron spoke of the
parties he had been to and the people he had met, the less
became William's resistance and the stronger the yearn-
ing to meet and become part of the groups Ron described.
When Ron told him about the invitation from Colin Ashworth, he could not hold out any longer and accepted.

"Let's join the others."

"No. I'll sit here for a little while longer. Perhaps
Margot will come back and we can continue our talk."

He was pathetically grateful for the friendliness of
Margot and the understanding shown by Colin Ashworth.
Ron looked at him with raised eyebrows, then left
him.

Another woman sank down beside him. It was the
woman he had dubbed "duchess." She gazed at him as if
he was some curio. She should have had a lorgnette, he
thought. Then she spoke: "Tell me, what do you do?"
her voice cool and condescending. Her tone and manner
chilled him and he felt an instant dislike.

"Do?" he asked.

"Yes!"

"I work in an office. I'm a"—He thought of saying
"clerk"—"messenger."

"I don't mean your type of work." Waving it aside as if
it was a distasteful object. "Do you paint or write? If I
like what you do, I can be very helpful."

"No."

"Come now. I bet that isn't true. The others, they do
either one or the other."

There was no need to ask who the others were and
whether she was one of the important people Ron had
told him about.

"I've told you the truth. I don't do a thing."

He was not worried about deceiving her. If she was to check with Ron it would be just too bad. She was not going to add him to her collection.

"You don't paint and you don't write and you're a messenger?" Her eyes and voice jabbed at him.

"That's right."

"Then what are you doing here?" she shot at him.

"The same thing you're doing." His dislike for her strengthened him, conquering the tremblings. "I'm here because I was invited."

"I don't want any of your damn cheek!" Voice jumping several octaves.

People on the couch and those nearby turned to stare.

She got up, nostrils flaring and breath drawn in audible snorts.

A horrified Ron pushed his way towards them.

"Mrs. Meredith, what is the matter?" he exclaimed. "What's happened?"

"I've been insulted by this impertinent messenger boy!" she said, pointing an accusing finger at William.

Ron faced him. "Get up and apologize at once!" he said, voice thick with reproach.

William looked at Ron, whose composure was crumbling with the effort to placate Mrs. Meredith. He was sick to the stomach at what he considered a betrayal on Ron's part, and his former unease gave way to anger.

She would have accepted him if he had told her that he too was a writer, and here was Ron, without checking, taking her part.

His admiration for Ron turned to contempt. He knew now why Ron had been so ingratiating. His talents and those of the others were on display like virgins for sale, to her and those like her, and Ron was their pimp.

It was for this that Ron snubbed his own—to walk in the shadow of a Mrs. Meredith—pushed them aside, forgetting that he too came from them. And this was what he had envied Ron for! The ability to converse and move with ease amongst them, to provide another virgin for their inspection. His anger brought a flood of blood to his head, making speech impossible as he glared at Ron. He got up from the couch and blindly pushed his way through the animated throng, unaware of the approval evident in Margot Pearce's eyes.

THE COMPLETE GENTLEMAN

Amos Tutuola

One of the most prolific African writers, Amos
Tutuola is the author of six books: *The Palm-Wine
Drinkard* (1952), *My Life in the Bush of Ghosts*
(1954), *Simbi and the Satyr of the Dark Jungle*
(1956), *The Brave African Huntress* (1958), *The
Feather Woman of the Jungle* (1962), and *Ajaiyi
and His Inherited Poverty* (1967). Tutuola, who
was born in Abeokuta, Western Nigeria, in 1920,
completed six years of primary school education,
which were followed by further training as a blacksmith. "The Complete Gentleman" is an excerpt
from his first work, *The Palm-Wine Drinkard*.

THE DESCRIPTION OF THE
CURIOUS CREATURE—

He was a beautiful "complete" gentleman, he dressed
with the finest and most costly clothes, all the parts of
his body were completed, he was a tall man but stout.
As this gentleman came to the market on that day, if he
had been an article or animal for sale, he would be sold at
least for £2000 (two thousand pounds). As this complete
gentleman came to the market on that day, and at the
same time that this lady saw him in the market, she did
nothing more than to ask him where he was living, but
this fine gentleman did not answer her or approach her
at all. But when she noticed that the fine or complete
gentleman did not listen to her, she left her articles and
began to watch the movements of the complete gentleman about in the market and left her articles unsold.

By and by the market closed for that day then the

whole people in the market were returning to their destinations etc., and the complete gentleman was returning to his own too, but as this lady was following him about in the market all the while, she saw him when he was returning to his destination as others did, then she was following him (complete gentleman) to an unknown place. But as she was following the complete gentleman along the road, he was telling her to go back or not to follow him, but the lady did not listen to what he was telling her, and when the complete gentleman had tired of telling her not to follow him or to go back to her town, he left her to follow him.

Do Not Follow Unknown Man's Beauty

But when they had travelled about twelve miles away from that market, they left the road on which they were travelling and started to travel inside an endless forest in which only the terrible creatures were living.

Return the Parts of Body to the Owners; Or Hired Parts of the Complete Gentleman's Body to Be Returned

As they were travelling along in this endless forest then the complete gentleman in the market that the lady was following, began to return the hired parts of his body to the owners and he was paying them the rentage money. When he reached where he hired the left foot, he pulled it out, he gave it to the owner and paid him, and they kept going; when they reached the place where he hired the right foot, he pulled it out and gave it to the owner and paid for the rentage. Now both feet had returned to the owners, so he began to crawl along on the ground, by that time, that lady wanted to go back to her town or her father, but the terrible and curious creature or the complete gentleman did not allow her to return or go back to her town or her father again and the complete gentleman said thus:—"I had told you not to follow me before we branched into this endless forest which belongs to only terrible and curious creatures, but when I became a half-bodied incomplete gentleman you wanted to go back, now that cannot be done, you have failed. Even you have never seen anything yet, just follow me."

When they went furthermore, then they reached where he hired the belly, ribs, chest etc., then he pulled them out and gave them to the owner and paid for the rentage.

Now to this gentleman or terrible creature remained only the head and both arms with neck, by that time he could not crawl as before but only went jumping on as a bull-frog and now this lady was soon faint for this fearful creature whom she was following. But when the lady saw every part of this complete gentleman in the market was spared or hired and he was returning them to the owners, then she began to try all her efforts to return to her father's town, but she was not allowed by this fearful creature at all.

When they reached where he hired both arms, he pulled them out and gave them to the owner, he paid for them; and they were still going on in this endless forest, they reached the place where he hired the neck, he pulled it out and gave it to the owner and paid for it as well.

A Full-Bodied Gentleman
Reduced to Head

Now this complete gentleman was reduced to head and when they reached where he hired the skin and flesh which covered the head, he returned them, and paid to the owner, now the complete gentleman in the market reduced to a "SKULL" and this lady remained with only "Skull." When the lady saw that she remained with only Skull, she began to say that her father had been telling her to marry a man, but she did not listen to or believe him.

When the lady saw that the gentleman became a Skull, she began to faint, but the Skull told her if she would die she would die and she would follow him to his house. But by the time that he was saying so, he was humming with a terrible voice and also grew very wild and even if there was a person two miles away he would not have to listen before hearing him, so this lady began to run away in that forest for her life, but the Skull chased her and within a few yards, he caught her, because he was very clever and smart as he was only Skull and he could jump a mile to the second before coming down. He caught the lady in this way: so when the lady was running away for her life, he hastily ran to her front and stopped her as a log of wood.

By and by, this lady followed the Skull to his house, and the house was a hole which was under the ground. When they reached there both of them entered the hole. But there were only Skulls living in that hole. At the same time that they entered the hole, he tied a single Cowrie on the neck of this lady with a kind of rope, after that, he gave her a large frog on which she sat as a stool, then he gave a whistle to a Skull of his kind to keep watch on this lady whenever she wanted to run away. Because the Skull knew already that the lady would attempt to run away from the hole. Then he went to the back yard to where his family were staying in the day time till night.

But one day, the lady attempted to escape from the hole, and at the same time that the Skull who was watching her whistled to the rest of the Skulls that were in the back yard, the whole of them rushed out to the place where the lady sat on the bullfrog, so they caught her, but as all of them were rushing out, they were rolling on the ground as if a thousand petrol drums were pushing along a hard road. After she was caught, then they brought her back to sit on the same frog as usual. If the Skull who was watching her fell asleep, and if the lady wanted to escape, the cowrie that was tied on her neck would raise up the alarm with a terrible noise, so that the Skull who was watching her would wake up at once and then the rest of the Skull's family would rush out from the back in thousands to the lady and ask her what she wanted to do with a curious and terrible voice.

But the lady could not talk at all, because as the cowrie had been tied on her neck, she became dumb at the same moment.

The Father of Gods Should Find Out Whereabouts the Daughter of the Head of the Town Was

Now as the father of the lady first asked for my name and I told him that my name was "Father of gods who could do anything in this world," then he told me that if I could find out where his daughter was and bring her to him, then he would tell me where my palm-wine tapster was. But when he said so, I was jumping up with gladness that he should promise me that he would tell me where my tapster was. I agreed to what he said; the father and parent of this lady never knew whereabouts their daughter was, but they had information that the lady followed a complete gentleman in the market. As I was the "Father of gods who could do anything in this world," when it was at night I sacrificed to my juju with a goat.

And when it was early in the morning, I sent for forty kegs of palm-wine. After I had drunk it all, I started to investigate whereabouts was the lady. As it was the market-day, I started the investigation from the market. But as I was a juju-man, I knew all the kinds of people in that market. When it was exactly 9 o'clock a.m., the very complete gentleman whom the lady followed came to the market again, and at the same time that I saw him, I knew that he was a curious and terrible creature.

The Lady Was Not to Be Blamed for Following the Skull as a Complete Gentleman

I could not blame the lady for following the Skull as a complete gentleman to his house at all. Because if I were a lady, no doubt I would follow him to wherever he would go, and still as I was a man I would jealous him more than that, because if this gentleman went to the battlefield, surely, enemy would not kill him or capture him and if bombers saw him in a town which was to be bombed, they would not throw bombs on his presence, and if they did throw it, the bomb itself would not explode until this gentleman would leave that town, because of his beauty. At the same time that I saw this gentleman in the market on that day, what I was doing was only to follow him about in the market. After I looked at him for so many hours, then I ran to a corner of the market and I cried for a few minutes because I thought within myself why was I not created with beauty as this gentleman, but when I remembered that he was only a Skull, then I thanked God that He had created me without beauty, so I went back to him in the market, but I was still attracted by his beauty. So when the market closed for that day, and when everybody was returning to his or her destination, this gentleman was returning to his own too and I followed him to know where he was living.

INVESTIGATION TO THE SKULL'S FAMILY'S HOUSE

When I travelled with him a distance of about twelve miles away to that market, the gentleman left the really road on which we were travelling and branched into an endless forest and I was following him, but as I did not want him to see that I was following him, then I used one of my juju which changed me into a lizard and followed him. But after I had travelled with him a distance of about twenty-five miles away in this endless forest, he began to pull out all the parts of his body and return them to the owners, and paid them.

After I had travelled with him for another fifty miles in this forest, then he reached his house and entered it, but I entered it also with him, as I was a lizard. The first thing that he did when he entered the hole (house) he went straight to the place where the lady was, and I saw the lady sat on a bullfrog with a single cowrie tied on her neck and a Skull who was watching her stood behind her. After he (gentleman) had seen that the lady was there, he went to the back yard where all his family were working.

THE INVESTIGATOR'S WONDERFUL WORK IN THE SKULL'S FAMILY'S HOUSE

When I saw this lady and when the Skull who brought her to that hole or whom I followed from the market to that hole went to the back yard, then I changed myself to a man as before, then I talked to the lady but she could not answer me at all, she only showed that she was in a serious condition. The Skull who was guarding her with a whistle fell asleep at that time.

To my surprise, when I helped the lady to stand up from the frog on which she sat, the cowrie that was tied on her neck made a curious noise at once, and when the Skull who was watching her heard the noise, he woke up and blew the whistle to the rest, then the whole of them rushed to the place and surrounded the lady and me, but at the same time that they saw me there, one of them ran to a pit which was not so far from that spot, the pit was filled with cowries. He picked one cowrie out of the pit, after that he was running towards me, and the whole crowd wanted to tie the cowrie on my neck too. But before they could do that, I had changed myself into air, they could not trace me out again, but I was looking at them. I believed that the cowries in that pit were their power and to reduce the power of any human being whenever tied on his or her neck and also to make a person dumb.

Over one hour after I had dissolved into air, these Skulls went back to the back yard, but there remained the Skull who was watching her.

After they had returned to the back yard, I changed to a man as usual, then I took the lady from the frog, but at the same time that I touched her, the cowrie which was tied on her neck began to shout; even if a person was four miles away he would not have to listen before hearing, but immediately the Skull who was watching her heard the noise and saw me when I took her from that frog, he blew the whistle to the rest of them who were in the back yard.

Immediately the whole Skull family heard the whistle when blew to them, they were rushing out to the place and before they could reach there, I had left their hole for the forest, but before I could travel about one hundred yards in the forest, they had rushed out from their hole to inside the forest and I was still running away with the lady. As these Skulls were chasing me about in the forest, they were rolling on the ground like large stones and also humming with terrible noise, but when I saw that they had nearly caught me or if I continued to run away like that, no doubt, they would catch me sooner, then I changed the lady to a kitten and put her inside my pocket and changed myself to a very small bird which I could describe as a "sparrow" in English language.

After that I flew away, but as I was flying in the sky, the cowrie which was tied on that lady's neck was still making a noise and I tried all my best to stop the noise, but all were in vain. When I reached home with the lady, I changed her to a lady as she was before and also myself changed to man as well. When her father saw that I brought his daughter back home, he was exceedingly glad and said thus:—"You are the 'Father of gods' as you had told me before."

But as the lady was now at home, the cowrie on her neck did not stop making a terrible noise once, and she could not talk to anybody; she showed only that she was very glad she was at home. Now I had brought the lady but she could not talk, eat or loose away the cowrie on her neck, because the terrible noise of the cowrie did not allow anybody to rest or sleep at all.

THERE REMAIN GREATER TASKS AHEAD

Now I began to cut the rope of the cowrie from her neck and to make her talk and eat, but all my efforts were in vain. At last I tried my best to cut off the rope of the cowrie; it only stopped the noise, but I was unable to loose it away from her neck.

When her father saw all my trouble, he thanked me greatly and repeated again that as I called myself "Father of gods who could do anything in this world" I ought to do the rest of the work. But when he said so, I was very ashamed and thought within myself that if I return to the Skulls' hole or house, they might kill me and the forest was very dangerous travel always, again I could not go directly to the Skulls in their hole and ask them how to loose away the cowrie which was tied on the lady's neck and to make her talk and eat.

BACK TO THE SKULL'S FAMILY'S HOUSE

On the third day after I had brought the lady to her father's house, I returned to the endless forest for further investigation. When there remained about one mile to reach the hole of these Skulls, there I saw the very Skull who the lady had followed from the market as a complete gentleman to the hole of Skull's family's house, and at the same time that I saw him like that, I changed into a liazrd and climbed a tree which was near him.

He stood before two plants, then he cut a single opposite leaf from the opposite plant; he held the leaf with his right hand and he was saying thus:—"As this lady was taken from me, if this opposite leaf is not given her to eat, she will not talk forever," after that he threw the leaf down on the ground. Then he cut another single compound leaf with his left hand and said that if this single compound is not given to this lady, to eat, the cowrie on her neck could not be loosened away forever and it would be making a terrible noise forever.

After he said so, he threw the leaf down at the same spot, then he jumped away. So after he had jumped very far away (luckily, I was there when he was doing all these things, and I saw the place that he threw both leaves separately), then I changed myself to a man as before, I went to the place that he threw both leaves, then I picked them up and I went home at once.

But at the same time that I reached home, I cooked both leaves separately and gave her to eat; to my surprise the lady began to talk at once. After that, I gave her the compound leaf to eat for the second time and immediately she ate that too, the cowrie which was tied on her neck by the Skull, loosened away by itself, but it disappeared at the same time. So when the father and mother saw the wonderful work which I had done for them, they brought fifty kegs of palm-wine for me, they gave me the lady as wife and two rooms in that house in which to live with them. So, I saved the lady from the complete gentleman in the market who was afterwards reduced to a Skull and the lady became my wife since that day. This was how I got a wife.

SARZAN

Birago Diop

Translated from the French by Ellen Conroy Kennedy

Birago Diop was born in Senegal in 1906. He received part of his education at the Lycée Faidherbe in St. Louis (in Senegal) and continued his studies in France, at the University of Toulouse, becoming a veterinary surgeon. After his return to Africa, he worked for a number of years as a veterinary officer at Ouagadougou (now a part of Upper Volta). "Sarzan" is undoubtedly a story based on those experiences. Diop is the author of several volumes of traditional folk stories: *Les Contes d'Amadou Koumba* (1947), *Les Nouveaux Contes d'Amadou Koumba* (1958), and *Contes et Lavanes* (1963). "Sarzan" is from the first of these volumes.

It was hard to distinguish the piles of ruins from the termite mounds, and only an ostrich shell, cracked and yellowed by the weather, still indicated at the tip of a tall column what once had been the *mirab* of the mosque El Hadj Omar's warriors had built. The Toucouleur conqueror had shorn the hair and shaved the heads of the forbears of those who are now the village elders. He had decapitated those who would not submit to Koranic law. Once again, the village elders wear their hair in braids. The sacred woods long ago burnt by the fanatic Talibés have long since grown tall again, and still harbor the cult objects, pots whitened from the boiling of millet or browned by the clotted blood of sacrificed chickens and dogs.

Like grain felled at random beneath the flail, or ripe

fruits that drop from branches filled with sap, whole families left Dougouba to form new villages, Dougoubanis. Some of the young people would go off to work in Segou, in Bamako, in Kayes, or Dakar; others went to work the Senegalese groundnut fields, returning when the harvest was in and the product had been shipped. All knew the root of their lives was still in Dougouba, which had long ago erased all traces of the Islamic hordes and returned to the teachings of the ancestors.

One son of Dougouba had ventured farther and for a longer time than any of the others: Thiemokho Keita.

From Dougouba he went to the local capital, from there to Kati, from Kati to Dakar, from Dakar to Casablanca, from Casablanca to Frejus, and then to Damascus. Leaving the Sudan to be a soldier, Thiemokho Keita had been trained in Senegal, fought in Morocco, stood guard in France, and patrolled in Lebanon. He returned to Dougouba a sergeant, catching a lift in my medical caravan.

I had been making my veterinarian's rounds in the heart of the Sudan when I met Sergeant Keita in a local administrator's office. He had just been discharged from the service and wanted to enlist in the local police, or to be taken on as an interpreter.

"No," the local commandant told him. "You can do more for the administration by returning to your village. You who have travelled so much and seen so much, you can teach the others something about how white men live. You'll 'civilize' them a bit. Say there, Doctor," he continued, turning to me, "since you're going in that direction, won't you take Keita with you? It will spare him the wear and tear of the road and save him some time. It's fifteen years he's been gone."

So we set out. The driver, the sergeant and I occupied the front seat of the little truck, while behind, the cooks, medical aides, driver's helper and the civil guard were crowded together among the field kitchen, the camp bed and the cases of serum and vaccine. The sergeant told me about his life as a soldier, then as a noncommissioned officer. I heard about the Riff Wars from the viewpoint of a Sudanese rifleman; he talked about Marseille, Toulon, Frejus, Beirut. He seemed no longer to see the road in front of us. Rough as a corrugated tin room, it was paved with logs covered with a layer of clay, disintegrating into dust now because of the torrid heat and the extreme dryness. It was an unctuous oily dust that stuck to our faces like a yellow mask, making our teeth gritty and screening from our view the chattering baboons and frightened does that leaped about in our wake. Through the choking haze, Keita seemed to see once more the minarets of Fez, the teeming crowds of Marseille, the great tall buildings of France, the blue sea.

By noon we reached the town of Madougou, where the road ended. To reach Dougouba by nightfall, we took horses and bearers.

"When you come back this way again," Keita said, "you'll go all the way to Dougouba by car. Tomorrow I'm going to get started on a road."

The muffled rolling of a tom-tom announced that we were nearing the village. A grey mass of huts appeared, topped by the darker grey of three palm trees against a paler grey sky. The rumbling was accompanied now by the sharp sound of three notes on a flute. We were in Dougouba. I got down first and asked for the village chief.

"*Dougou-tigui*, here is your son, the Sergeant Keita."

Thiemokho Keita jumped down from his horse. As if the sound of his shoes on the ground had been a signal, the drumming stopped and the flute was silent. The aged chief took Keita's two hands while other old men examined his arms, his shoulders, his decorations. Some old women ran up and began fingering the puttees at his knees. Tears shone on the dark faces, settling in the wrinkles that crossed their ritual scars. Everyone was saying:

"Keita, Keita, Keita!"

"Those," the old man quavered at last, "those who brought your steps back to our village on this day are generous and good."

It was in fact a day unlike other days in Dougouba. It was the day of the Kotéba, the day of the Testing.

The drum resumed its rumbling, pierced by the sharp whistles of the flute. Inside the circle of women, children, and grown men, bare-chested youngsters, each carrying a long branch of balazan wood, stripped clean and supple as a whip, were turning about to the rhythm of the tom-tom. In the center of this moving circle, crouching with his knees and elbows on the ground, the flute player gave forth three notes, always the same. Above him a young man would come to stand, legs apart, arms spread in the shape of a cross, while the others, passing close to him, let their whips whistle. The blows fell on his chest, leaving a stripe wide as a thumb, sometimes breaking the skin. The sharp voice of the flute would go a note higher, the tom-tom would grow softer, as the whips whistled and the blood ran. Firelight gleamed on the black-brown body and light from the embers leaped to the tops of the palm trees, softly creaking in the evening wind. Kotéba! the test of endurance, the testing for insensibility to pain. The child who cries when he hurts himself is only a child; the child who cries when he is hurt will not make a man.

Kotéba! to offer one's back, receive the blow, turn around and give it back to someone else. Kotéba!

"This, these are still the ways of savages!"

I turned round, it was Sergeant Keita who had come to join me by the drum.

The ways of savages? This testing, which among other things produced men who were hard and tough! What was it that had enabled the forbears of these youngsters to march with enormous burdens on their heads for whole days without stopping? What had made Thiemokho Keita himself, and others like him, able to fight valiantly beneath skies where the sun itself is very often sickly, to labor with heavy packs on their backs, enduring cold, thirst, and hunger?

The ways of savages? Perhaps. But I was thinking that elsewhere, where I came from, we had left these initiations behind. For our adolescents there was no longer a "house of men" where the body, the mind and the character were tempered; where the ancient *passines*, the riddles and conundrums, were learned by dint of beatings on the bent back and the held-out fingers, and where the *kassaks*, the age-old memory training songs whose words and wisdom descend to us from the dark nights, were assured their place in our heads by the heat of live coals that burned the palms of our hands. I was thinking that as far as I could see we had still gained nothing, that perhaps we had left these old ways behind without having caught up with the new ones.

The tom-tom murmured on, sustaining the piercing voice of the flute. The fires died and were born again. I went to the hut that had been prepared for me. Inside, mixed with the thick smell of *banco*—the dried clay kneaded with broken rotten straw that made the hut rainproof—a subtler odor hung, the fragrance of the dead, whose number, three, was indicated by animal horns fixed to the wall at the level of a man's height. For, in Dougouba, the cemetery too had disappeared, and the dead continued to live with the living. They were buried in the huts.

The sun was already warm when I took my leave, but Dougouba was still asleep: drunk, both from fatigue and from the millet beer that had circulated in calabashes from hand to mouth and mouth to hand the whole night long.

"Good bye," said Keita. "The next time you come there will be a road, I promise you."

The work in other sectors and localities kept me from returning to Dougouba until the following year.

It was late in the afternoon after a hard journey. The
air seemed a thick mass, hot and sticky, that we pushed
our way through with great effort.

Sergeant Keita had kept his word; the road went all the
way to Dougouba. As in all the villages at the sound of
the car a swarm of naked children appeared at the end
of the road, their little bodies grey-white with dust, and
on their heels came the reddish-brown dogs with cropped
ears and bony flanks. In the midst of the children a man
was gesticulating, waving a cow's tail attached to his right
wrist. When the car stopped, I saw it was the sergeant,
Thiemokho Keita. He wore a faded fatigue jacket, without
buttons or stripes. Underneath were a *boubou* and pants
made of strips of khaki-colored cotton, like the ones worn
by the village elders. His pants stopped above the knee
and were held together with pieces of string. His puttees
were in rags. He was barefoot but wore a *képi* on his head.

"Keita!"

The children scattered like a volley of sparrows, chirping:

"Ayi! Ayi!" (No! No!)

Thiemokho Keita did not take my hand. He looked at
me, but seemed not to see me. His gaze was so distant
that I couldn't help turning around to see what his eyes
were fixed upon through mine. Suddenly, agitating his
cowtail, he began to cry out in a hoarse voice:

> Listen to things
> More often than beings
> Hear the voice of fire
> Hear the voice of water
> Listen in the wind to
> the sighs of the bush
> This is the ancestors breathing.

"He's mad," said my driver, whom I silenced with a
gesture. The sergeant was still chanting, in a strange,
sing-song voice:

SARZAN 63

Those who are dead are not ever gone
They are in the darkness that grows lighter
And in the darkness that grows darker
The dead are not down in the earth
They are in the trembling of the trees
In the moaning of the woods
In the water that runs
In the water that sleeps
They are in the hut, they are in the crowd.

The dead are not dead.
Listen to things
More often than beings
Hear the voice of fire
Hear the voice of water
Listen in the wind
To the bush that is sighing
This is the breathing of ancestors
Who have not gone away
Who are not under earth
Who are not really dead.

Those who are dead are not ever gone
They are in a woman's breast
In a child's wailing
and the log burning
in the moaning rock and
in the weeping grasses
in the forest in the home
The dead are not dead.

Hear the fire speak
Hear the water speak
Listen in the wind to
the bush that is sobbing
This is the ancestors breathing.

Each day they renew ancient bonds
Ancient bonds that hold fast

Binding our lot to their law
To the will of the spirits stronger than we are
Whose covenant binds us to life
Whose authority binds to their will
The will of the spirits that move
In the bed of the river, on the banks of the river
The breathing of ancestors
Wailing in the rocks and weeping in the grasses.

Spirits inhabit
the darkness that lightens, the darkness that darkens
the quivering tree, the murmuring wood
the running and the sleeping waters
Spirits much stronger than we are
The breathing of the dead who are not really dead
Of the dead who are not really gone
Of the dead now no more in the earth.

Listen to things
More often than beings. . . .

The children returned, circling round the old chief and the village elders. After the greetings, I asked what had happened to Sergeant Keita.

"Ayi! Ayi!" said the old men. "Ayi! Ayi!" echoed the children.

"No, not Keita!" said the old father, "Sarzan,* just Sarzan. We must not rouse the anger of the departed. Sarzan is no longer a Keita. The Dead and the Spirits have punished him for his offenses."

It had begun the day after his arrival, the very day of my departure from Dougouba.

Sergeant Keita had wanted to keep his father from sacrificing a white chicken to thank the ancestors for having brought him home safe and sound. Keita declared

* A Senegalese pronunciation of *sergent*, the French for sergeant—Trans.

that if he had come home it was quite simply that he had had to, and that the ancestors had had nothing to do with it.

"Leave the dead be," he had said. "They can no longer do anything for the living."

The old chief had paid no attention and the chicken had been sacrificed.

When it was time to work the fields, Thiemokho had called it useless and even stupid to kill black chickens and pour their blood into a corner of the fields. The work, he said, was enough. Rain would fall if it was going to. The millet, corn, groundnuts, yams and beans would grow all by themselves, and would grow better if the villagers would use the plows the local administrator had sent him. Keita cut down and burned the branches of Dassiri, the sacred tree, protector of the village and the cultivated fields, at whose foot the dogs were sacrificed.

On the day when the little boys were to be circumcised and the little girls excised,* Sergeant Keita had leaped upon their teacher, the Gangourang, who was dancing and chanting. He tore off the porcupine quills the Gangourang wore upon his head, and the netting that hid his body. From the head of Mama Djombo, the venerable grandfather who taught the young girls, Keita had ripped the cone-shaped yellow headdress topped with gri-gri charms and ribbons. All this he called "the ways of savages." And yet he had been to Nice, and seen the carnival with the funny and frightening masks. The Whites, the Toubabs, it is true, wore masks for fun and not in order to teach their children the wisdom of the ancients.

Sergeant Keita had unhooked the little bag hanging in his hut which held the Nyanaboli, the Keita family spirit, and had thrown it into the yard, where the skinny dogs nearly won it from the children before the chief could get there.

* Female circumcision—Ed.

One morning he had gone into the sacred wood and broken the pots of boiled millet and sour milk. He had pushed over the little statues and pulled up the forked stakes tipped with hardened blood and chicken feathers. "The ways of savages," he called them. The sergeant, however, had been in churches. He had seen little statues there of saints and the Holy Virgins that people burned candles to. These statues, it is true, were covered with gilt and painted in bright colors—blues, reds and yellows. Certainly they were more beautiful than the blackened pygmies with long arms and short legs carved of cailcedrat or ebony that inhabited the sacred forest.

"You'll civilize them a bit," the local administrator had said. Sergeant Thiemokho Keita was going to "civilize" his people. It was necessary to break with tradition, do away with the beliefs upon which the village life, the existence of the families, the people's behavior had always rested. Superstition had to be eradicated. The ways of savages. Ways of savages, the hard treatment inflicted on the young initiates at circumcision to open their minds, form their character and teach them that nowhere, at any moment of their lives, can they, will they ever be alone. A way of savages, the Kotéba, which forges real men on whom pain can hold no sway. The ways of savages, the sacrifices, the blood offered to the ancestors and the earth . . . the boiling of millet and curdled milk poured out to the wandering spirits and the protective genies . . . the ways of savages.

All this Sergeant Keita proclaimed to the young and old of the village, standing in the shade of the palaver-tree.

It was nearly sunset when Thiemokho Keita went out of his mind. He was leaning against the palaver-tree, talking, talking, talking, against the medicine man who had sacrificed some dogs that very morning, against the old who didn't want to hear him, against the young who still listened to the old. He was still speaking, when suddenly

he felt something like a prick on his left shoulder. He
turned his head. When he looked at his listeners again,
his eyes were no longer the same. A white, foamy spittle
appeared at the corners of his mouth. He spoke, but it
was no longer the same words that emerged from his lips.
The spirits had taken his mind, and now they cried out
their fear:

> Black night! Black night!

He called at nightfall, and the women and children
trembled in their huts:

> Black night! Black night!

he cried at daybreak:

> Black night! Black night!

he howled at high noon. Night and day the spirits and
the genies and the ancestors made him speak, cry out and
chant. . . .

It was only at dawn that I was able to doze off in the
hut where the dead lived. All night I had heard Sergeant
Keita coming and going, howling, weeping, and singing:

> Trumpeting elephants hoot
> In the darkening wood
> Above the cursèd drums,
> Black night, black night!
>
> Milk sours in the calabash
> Gruel hardens in the jar
> And fear stalks in the hut,
> Black night, black night!
>
> The torches throw
> Bodiless flames
> In the air
> And then, quietly, glarelessly
> Smoke,
> Black night, black night!
>
> Restless spirits
> Meander and moan

Muttering lost words,
Words that strike fear,
Black night, black night!

From the chicken's chilled bodies
Or the warm moving corpse
Not a drop of blood runs
Neither black blood nor red,
Black night, black night!
Trumpeting elephants hoot
Above the cursèd drums,
Black night, black night!

Orphaned, the river calls out
In fear for the people
Endlessly, fruitlessly wandering
Far from its desolate banks,
Black night, black night!

And in the savannah, forlorn
Deserted by ancestors' spirits
The trumpeting elephants hoot
Above the cursèd drums,
Black night, black night!

Sap freezes in the anxious trees
In trunks and leaves
That no longer can pray
To the ancestors haunting their feet,
Black night, black night!

Fear lurks in the hut
In the smoking torch
In the orphaned river
In the weary, soulless forest
In the anxious, faded trees

Trumpeting elephants hoot
In the darkening woods

Above the cursèd drums,
Black night, black night!

No one dared call him by his name any more, for the
spirits and the ancestors had made another man of him.
Thiemokho Keita was gone for the villagers. Only "Sarzan" was left, Sarzan-the-Mad.

THE WINNER

Barbara Kimenye

Barbara Kimenye is well known in East Africa as
a journalist. She is Ugandan and the author of two
collections of short stories: *Kalasanda* (1965) and
Kalasanda Revisited (1965). "The Winner" is from
the first of these.

When Pius Ndawula won the football pools, overnight
he seemed to become the most popular man in Buganda.
Hosts of relatives converged upon him from the four
corners of the kingdom: cousins and nephews, nieces and
uncles, of whose existence he had never before been
aware, turned up in Kalasanda by the busload, together
with crowds of individuals who, despite their downtrodden
appearance, assured Pius that they and they alone were
capable of seeing that his money was properly invested—
preferably in their own particular businesses! Also lurking
around Pius's unpretentious mud hut were newspaper reporters, slick young men weighed down with cameras and
sporting loud checked caps or trilbies set at conspicuously
jaunty angles, and serious young men from Radio Uganda
who were anxious to record Pius's delight at his astonish-
ing luck for the edification of the Uganda listening public.

The rest of Kalasanda were so taken by surprise that they could only call and briefly congratulate Pius before being elbowed out of the way by his more garrulous relations. All, that is to say, except Pius's greatest friend Salongo, the custodian of the Ssabalangira's tomb. He came and planted himself firmly in the house, and nobody attempted to move him. Almost blind, and very lame, he had tottered out with the aid of a stout stick. Just to see him arrive had caused a minor sensation in the village, for he hadn't left the tomb for years. But recognizing at last a chance to house Ssabalangira's remains in a state befitting his former glory, made the slow, tortuous journey worthwhile to Salongo.

Nantondo hung about long enough to have her picture taken with Pius. Or rather, she managed to slip beside him just as the cameras clicked, and so it was that every Uganda newspaper, on the following day, carried a front-page photograph of "Mr. Pius Ndawula and his happy wife," a caption that caused Pius to shake with rage and threaten legal proceedings, but over which Nantondo gloated as she proudly showed it to everybody she visited.

"Tell us, Mr. Ndawula, what do you intend to do with all the money you have won . . . ?"

"Tell us, Mr. Ndawula, how often have you completed pools coupons . . . ?"

"Tell us . . . Tell us . . . Tell us . . ."

Pius's head was reeling under this bombardment of questions, and he was even more confused by Salongo's constant nudging and muttered advice to "Say nothing!" Nor did the relatives make things easier. Their persistent clamoring for his attention, and the way they kept shoving their children under his nose, made it impossible for him to think, let alone talk.

It isn't at all easy, when you have lived for sixty-five years in complete obscurity, to adjust yourself in a matter of hours to the role of a celebrity, and the strain was beginning to tell.

Behind the hut—Pius had no proper kitchen—gallons of tea were being boiled, whilst several of the female cousins were employed in ruthlessly hacking down the bunches of *matoke* from his meagre plantains, to cook food for everybody. One woman—she had introduced herself as Cousin Sarah—discovered Pius's hidden store of banana beer, and dished it out to all and sundry as though it were her own. Pius had become very wary of Cousin Sarah. He didn't like the way in which she kept loudly remarking that he needed a woman about the place, and he was even more seriously alarmed when suddenly Salongo gave him a painful dig in the ribs and muttered, "You'll have to watch that one—she's a sticker!"

Everybody who came wanted to see the telegram that announced Pius's win. When it had arrived at the Ggombolola Headquarters—the postal address of everyone residing within a radius of fifteen miles—Musisi had brought it out personally, delighted to be the bearer of such good tidings. At Pius's request he had gone straight away to tell Salongo, and then back to his office to send an acknowledgement on behalf of Pius to the pools firm, leaving the old man to dream rosy dreams. An extension of his small coffee *shamba*, a new roof on his house—or maybe an entirely new house—concrete blocks this time, with a verandah perhaps. Then there were hens. Salongo and he had always said there was money in hens these days, now that the women ate eggs and chicken; not that either of them agreed with the practice. Say what you liked, women who ate chicken and eggs were fairly asking to be infertile! That woman Welfare Officer who came round snooping occasionally, tried to say it was all nonsense, that chicken meat and eggs made bigger and better babies. Well, they might look bigger and better, but nobody could deny that they were fewer! Which only goes to show.

But news spreads fast in Africa—perhaps the newspapers have contacts in the pools offices. Anyway, before the telegram had even reached Pius, announcements were appearing in the local newspapers, and Pius was still quietly lost in his private dreams when the first batch of visitors arrived. At first he was at a loss to understand what was happening. People he hadn't seen for years and only recognised with difficulty fell upon him with cries of joy. "Cousin Pius, the family are delighted!" "Cousin Pius, why have you not visited us all this time?"

Pius was pleased to see his nearest and dearest gathered around him. It warmed his old heart once more to find himself in the bosom of his family, and he welcomed them effusively. The second crowd to arrive were no less well received, but there was a marked coolness on the part of their forerunners.

However, as time had gone by and the flood of strange faces had gained momentum, Pius's *shamba* had come to resemble a political meeting. All to be seen from the door of the house was a turbulent sea of white *kanzus* and brilliant *busutis*, and the house itself was full of people and tobacco smoke.

The precious telegram was passed from hand to hand until it was reduced to a limp fragment of paper with the lettering partly obliterated: not that it mattered very much, for only a few members of the company could read English.

"Now, Mr. Ndawula, we are ready to take the recording." The speaker was a slight young man wearing a checked shirt. "I shall ask you a few questions, and you simply answer me in your normal voice." Pius looked at the leather box with its two revolving spools, and licked his lips. "Say nothing!" came a hoarse whisper from Salongo. The young man steadfastly ignored him, and went ahead in his best BBC manner. "Well, Mr. Ndawula, first of all let me congratulate you on your winning the pools. Would you like to tell our listeners what it feels like suddenly to find yourself rich?" There was an uncomfortable pause, during which Pius stared mesmerised at the racing spools and the young man tried frantically to span the gap by asking "I mean, have you any plans for the future?" Pius swallowed audibly, and opened his mouth to say something, but shut it again when Salongo growled, "Tell him nothing!"

The young man snapped off the machine, shaking his head in exasperation. "Look here, sir, all I want you to do is to say something—I'm not asking you to make a speech! Now, I'll tell you what. I shall ask you again what it feels like suddenly to come into money, and you say something like 'It was a wonderful surprise, and naturally I feel very pleased'—and will you ask your friend not to interrupt! Got it? Okay, off we go!"

The machine was again switched on, and the man brightly put his question, "Now, Mr. Ndawula, what does it feel like to win the pools?" Pius swallowed, then quickly chanted in a voice all off key, "It was a wonderful surprise and naturally I feel very happy and will you ask your friend not to interrupt!" The young man nearly wept. This happened to be his first assignment as a radio interviewer, and it looked like being his last. He switched off the machine and mourned his lusterless future, groaning. At that moment Cousin Sarah caught his eye. "Perhaps I can help you," she said. "I am Mr. Ndawula's cousin." She made this pronouncement in a manner that suggested Pius had no others. The young man brightened considerably. "Well, madam, if you could tell me something about Mr. Ndawula's plans, I would be most grateful." Cousin Sarah folded her arms across her imposing bosom, and when the machine again started up, she was off. Yes, Mr. Ndawula was very happy about the money. No, she didn't think he had any definite plans on how to spend it—with all these people about he didn't have time to think. Yes, Mr. Ndawula lived completely alone, but she was prepared to stay and look after him for as long as he needed her. Here a significant glance passed between the other women in the room, who clicked their teeth and let out long "Eeeeeeehs!" of incredulity. Yes, she believed she was Mr. Ndawula's nearest living relative by marriage . . .

Pius listened to her confident aplomb with growing horror, whilst Salongo frantically nudged him and whispered, "There! What did I tell you! That woman's a sticker!"

Around three in the afternoon, *matoke* and tea were served, the *matoke*, on wide fresh plantain leaves, since Pius owned only three plates, and the tea in anything handy—tin cans, old jars, etc.—because he was short of cups too. Pius ate very little, but he was glad of the tea. He had shaken hands with so many people that his arm ached, and he was tired of the chatter and the comings and goings in his house of all these strangers. Most of all he was tired of Cousin Sarah, who insisted on treating him like an idiot invalid. She kept everybody else at bay, as far as she possibly could, and when one woman plonked a sticky fat baby on his lap, Cousin Sarah dragged the child away as though it were infectious. Naturally, a few cross words were exchanged between Sarah and the fond mother, but by this time Pius was past caring.

Yosefu Mukasa and Kibuka called in the early evening, when some of the relatives were departing with effusive promises to come again tomorrow. They were both alarmed at the weariness they saw on Pius's face. The old man looked utterly worn out, his skin grey and sickly. Also, they were a bit taken aback by the presence of Cousin Sarah, who pressed them to take tea and behaved in every respect as though she were mistress of the house. "I believe my late husband knew you very well, sir," she told Yosefu. "He used to be a Miruka chief in Buyaga County. His name was Kivumbi." "Ah, yes," Yosefu replied, "I remember Kivumbi very well indeed. We often hunted together. I was sorry to hear of his death. He was a good man." Cousin Sarah shrugged her shoulders. "Yes, he was a good man. But what the Lord giveth, He also taketh away." Thus was the late Kivumbi dismissed from the conversation.

Hearing all this enabled Pius to define the exact relationship between himself and Cousin Sarah, and even by Kiganda standards it was virtually nonexistent, for the late Kivumbi had been the stepson of one of Pius's cousins.

"Your stroke of luck seems to have exhausted you, Pius," Kibuka remarked, when he and Yosefu were seated on the rough wooden chairs brough forth by Cousin Sarah.

Salongo glared at the world in general and snarled, "Of course he is exhausted! Who wouldn't be with all these scavengers collected to pick his bones?" Pius hushed him as one would a child. "No, no, Salongo. It is quite natural that my family should gather round me at a time like this. Only I fear I am perhaps a little too old for all this excitement."

Salongo spat expertly through the open doorway, narrowly missing a group of guests who were preparing to bed down, and said, "That woman doesn't think he's too old. She's out to catch him. I've seen her type elsewhere!"

Yosefu's mouth quirked with amusement at the thought that "elsewhere" could only mean the Ssabalangira's tomb, which Salongo had guarded for the better part of his adult life. "Well, she's a fine woman," he remarked. "But see here, Pius," he went on, "don't be offended by my proposal, but wouldn't it be better if you came and stayed with us at Mutunda for tonight? Miriamu would love to have you, and you look as though you need a good night's rest, which you wouldn't get here —those relatives of yours outside are preparing a fire and are ready to dance the night away!"

"I think that's a wonderful idea!" said Cousin Sarah, bouncing in to remove the tea cups. "You go with Mr.

Mukasa, Cousin Pius. The change will do you as much good as the rest. And don't worry about your home—I shall stay here and look after things." Pius hesitated. "Well, I think I shall be all right here—I don't like to give Miriamu any extra work. . . ." Salongo muttered. "Go to Yosefu's. You don't want to be left alone in the house with that woman—there's no knowing what she might get up to. . . !" "I'll pack a few things for you, Pius," announced Cousin Sarah and bustled off before anything more could be said, pausing only long enough to give Salongo a look that was meant to wither him on the spot.

So Pius found himself being driven away to Mutunda in Yosefu's car, enjoying the pleasant sensation of not having to bother about a thing. Salongo too had been given a lift to as near the tomb as the car could travel, and his wizened old face was contorted into an irregular smile, for Pius had promised to help him build a new house for the Ssabalangira. For him the day had been well spent, despite Cousin Sarah.

Pius spent an enjoyable evening with the Mukasas. They had a well-cooked supper, followed by a glass of cool beer as they sat back and listened to the local news on the radio. Pius had so far relaxed as to tell the Mukasas modestly that he had been interviewed by Radio Uganda that morning, and when Radio Newsreel was announced they waited breathlessly to hear his voice. But instead of Pius, Cousin Sarah came booming over the air. Until that moment the old man had completely forgotten the incident of the tape-recording. In fact, he had almost forgotten Cousin Sarah. Now it all came back to him with a shiver of apprehension. Salongo was right. That woman did mean business! It was a chilling thought. However, it didn't cause him to lose any sleep. He slept like a cherub, as if he hadn't a care in the world.

Because he looked so refreshed in the morning, Miriamu insisted on keeping him at Mutunda for another day. "I know you feel better, but after seeing you yesterday, I think a little holiday with us will do you good. Go home tomorrow, when the excitement has died down a bit," she advised.

Soon after lunch, as Pius was taking a nap in a chair on the verandah, Musisi drove up in the landrover, with Cousin Sarah by his side. Miriamu came out to greet them, barely disguising her curiosity about the formidable woman about whom she had heard so much. The two women sized each other up and decided to be friends.

Meanwhile, Musisi approached the old man. "Sit down, son," Pius waved him to a chair at his side. "Miriamu feeds me so well it's all I can do to keep awake."

"I am glad you are having a rest, sir." Musisi fumbled in the pocket of his jacket. "There is another telegram for you. Shall I read it?" The old man sat up expectantly and said, "If you'll be so kind."

Musisi first read the telegram in silence, then he looked at Pius and commented, "Well, sir, I'm afraid it isn't good news."

"Not good news? Has somebody died?"

Musisi smiled. "Well, no. It isn't really as bad as that. The thing is, the pools firm say that owing to an unfortunate oversight they omitted to add, in the first telegram, that the prize money is to be shared among three hundred other people."

Pius was stunned. Eventually he murmured, "Tell me, how much does that mean I shall get?"

"Three hundred into seventeen thousand pounds won't give you much over a thousand shillings."

To Musisi's astonishment, Pius sat back and chuckled. "More than a thousand shillings!" he said. "Why, that's a lot of money!"

"But it's not, when you expected so much more!"

"I agree. And yet, son, what would I have done with all those thousands of pounds? I am getting past the age when I need a lot."

Miriamu brought a mat onto the verandah and she and Cousin Sarah made themselves comfortable near the men. "What a disappointment!" cried Miriamu, but Cousin Sarah sniffed and said, "I agree with Cousin Pius. He wouldn't know what to do with seventeen thousand pounds, and the family would be hanging round his neck forevermore!"

At mention of Pius's family, Musisi frowned. "I should warn you, sir, those relatives of yours have made a terrific mess of your *shamba*—your plantains have been stripped —and Mrs. Kivumbi here," nodding at Sarah, "was only just in time to prevent them digging up your sweet potatoes!"

"Yes, Cousin Pius," added Sarah. "It will take us some time to put the *shamba* back in order. They've trodden down a whole bed of young beans."

"Oh, dear," said Pius weakly. "This is dreadful news."

"Don't worry. They will soon disappear when I tell them there is no money, and then I shall send for a couple of my grandsons to come and help us do some replanting." Pius could not help but admire the way Sarah took things in her stride.

Musisi rose from his chair. "I'm afraid I can't stay any longer, so I will go now and help Cousin Sarah clear the crowd, and see you tomorrow to take you home." He and Sarah climbed back into the landrover and Sarah waved energetically until the vehicle was out of sight.

"Your cousin is a fine woman," Miriamu told Pius, before going indoors. Pius merely grunted, but for some odd reason he felt the remark to be a compliment to himself.

All was quiet at Pius's home when Musisi brought him home next day. He saw at once that his *shamba* was well-nigh wrecked, but his drooping spirits quickly revived when Sarah placed a mug of steaming tea before him, and sat on a mat at his feet, explaining optimistically how matters could be remedied. Bit by bit he began telling her what he planned to do with the prize money, ending with, "Of course, I shan't be able to do everything now, especially since I promised Salongo something for the tomb."

Sarah poured some more tea and said, "Well, I think the roof should have priority. I noticed last night that there are several leaks. And whilst we're about it, it would be a good idea to build another room on and a small outside kitchen. Mud and wattle is cheap enough, and then the whole place can be plastered. You can still go ahead and extend your coffee. And as for hens, well, I have six good layers at home, as well as a fine cockerel. I'll bring them over!"

Pius looked at her in silence for a long time. She is a fine looking woman, he thought, and that blue *busuti* suits her. Nobody would ever take her for a grandmother—but why is she so anxious to throw herself at me?

"You sound as if you are planning to come and live here," he said at last, trying hard to sound casual.

Sarah turned to face him and replied, "Cousin Pius, I shall be very frank with you. Six months ago my youngest son got married and brought his wife to live with me. She's a very nice girl, but somehow I can't get used to having another woman in the house. My other son is in Kampala, and although I know I would be welcome there, he too has a wife, and three children, so if I went there I wouldn't be any better off. When I saw that bit about you in the paper, I suddenly remembered—although I don't expect you to—how you were at my wedding and so helpful to everybody. Well, I thought to myself, here is somebody who needs a good housekeeper, who needs somebody to keep the leeches off, now that he has come into money. I came along right away to take a look at you, and I can see I did the right thing. You do need me." She hesitated for a moment, and then said, "Only you might prefer to stay alone . . . I'm so used to having my own way, I never thought about that before."

Pius cleared his throat. "You're a very impetuous woman," was all he could find to say.

A week later, Pius wandered out to the tomb and found Salongo busily polishing the Ssabalangira's weapons. "I thought you were dead," growled the custodian, "it is so long since you came here—but then, this tomb thrives on neglect. Nobody cares that one of Buganda's greatest men lies here."

"I have been rather busy," murmured Pius. "But I didn't forget my promise to you. Here! I've brought you a hundred shillings, and I only wish it could have been more. At least it will buy a few cement blocks."

Salongo took the money and looked at it as if it were crawling with lice. Grudgingly he thanked Pius and then remarked, "Of course, you will find life more expensive now that you are keeping a woman in the house."

"I suppose Nantondo told you," Pius smiled sheepishly.

"Does it matter who told me?" the custodian replied. "Anyway, never say I didn't warn you. Next thing she'll want will be a ring marriage!"

Pius gave an uncertain laugh. "As a matter of fact, one of the reasons I came up here was to invite you to the wedding—it's next month."

Salongo carefully laid down the spear he was rubbing upon a piece of clean barkcloth and stared at his friend as if he had suddenly grown another head. "What a fool you are! And all this stems from your scribbling noughts and crosses on a bit of squared paper! I knew it would bring no good! At your age you ought to have more sense. Well, all I can advise is that you run while you still have the chance!"

For a moment Pius was full of misgivings. Was he, after all, behaving like a fool? Then he thought of Sarah, and the wonders she had worked with his house and his *shamba* in the short time they had been together. He felt reassured. "Well, I'm getting married, and I expect to see you at both the church and the reception, and if you don't appear, I shall want to know the reason why!" He was secretly delighted at the note of authority in his voice, and Salongo's face was the picture of astonishment. "All right," he mumbled, "I shall try and come. Before you go, cut a bunch of bananas to take back to your good lady, and there might be some cabbage ready at the back. I suppose I've got to hand it to her! She's the real winner!"

The Dark Room

Sylvain Bemba

Translated from the French by Robert Baldick

The French version of "The Dark Room" won
the Prix de la Nouvelle Africaine in 1964 and was
published at that time in *Preuves*. Sylvain Bemba
was born in the Congo and is currently chief editor of L'Agence Congolaise d'Information, Brazza-
ville.

I didn't say I liked him: I said I was fascinated by him.—
OSCAR WILDE

N'Toko liked taking his hairy face, the face of a
bearded, grimacing faun, round the streets of Paris. He
was conscious of his ugliness and he derived a sort of
secret pleasure from displaying his repulsive features with
calm effrontery. He was visibly amused by the shuddering
amazement which he caused in the street when he passed
other people who turned round to watch the huge Negro
walking away. Baggy clothes gave him an outline which
was vague, unfinished, blurred, almost ghostly. And yet,
when people came to know him better, they were surprised
to find that they no longer felt the slightest malaise in his
presence. Then they recognized that he had a certain
charm, an irresistible magnetism. . . .

N'Toko loved Paris. He still remembered his first days
in the famous city. On his arrival he had been disap-
pointed. He had expected to find a *de luxe* work in a

handsome gilded binding. Instead, a dismal, dirty sky and sad-looking walls showed him Paris in the guise of an old book found in a box on the quays. The miracle occurred when he began leafing through the worn volume. On every page, at every line, he met the hypnotic gaze of the statues' vacant eyes. He lived again through those centuries of a history which he had learnt at school and whose tide still beat in foaming breakers against the cliffs of modern times.

The first joys N'Toko experienced in Paris were those of a conquistador. He was discovering a new world. In his imagination he deliberately mixed up the over-familiar monuments of the capital. He wanted to discover his own Paris. His first monument was five feet seven inches high; surmounted by a peaked cap, it was handing back to absent-minded passers-by the way they had lost. Soon he rediscovered with the joy of an old inhabitant a familiar monument rising to a height of about five feet three inches, irrigated by two great rivers, coffee and good wine, exporting on a generous scale voluble words and sweeping gestures, and content with life. Then he conceived a passion for the *Métro*. He saw it as a symbol of physical love and pictured Paris in an indecent posture whenever the underground lament of the two frenzied lovers came faintly to his ears. A little later, his monuments became talking dolls which laughed idiotically at the slightest touch and repeated the same things like a gramophone needle stuck in the groove of a worn-out record. He amused himself by savaging these dolls, rather like a child who will not stop until he has destroyed the new toy whose mechanism he has been trying to understand. And in fact, he regarded his temporary homeland as a gigantic toy which he was trying to take to pieces with a vague feeling that he must revenge himself. On whom, on what? The answer was sleeping somewhere in his subconscious. . . .

Once again N'Toko stood up and walked unsteadily

towards the juke-box which was shining with all its chromium. He stopped in front of the machine and began methodically turning out his pockets. Seen from a distance, he seemed a defenceless figure confronting some threatening animal. Finally he found a coin, examined it carefully and inserted it in a slot. A sort of vague din filled the air. It reminded him of the dirges of the women mourners in his own country. Out there, they offered their services free of charge to bereaved families. Each mourner used the mental picture of a dead relation to produce a tearful expression, praising the merits of the deceased in a voice choking with sobs, and thus diverting her river of tears towards the family she was assisting.

This produced exactly the same result as the jam session which seemed to be welling up from the bowels of the huge music box.

Perched on stools, two women who looked like fashion models exchanged a brief glance.

"That record is beginning to get on my nerves," one of them said in a low voice. "That's probably the fiftieth time he's played it this afternoon."

"You know what I think?" replied the other, who had a more practical turn of mind. "I think that the client is ripe to work on now. I wouldn't have spoken to him for anything when he came in here, he looked so fierce. But I think I'll try him now."

"Be careful," the first woman said in a confidential tone of voice; "the fellow still doesn't strike me as easy to handle, and you risk working for nothing."

Through a hazy screen N'Toko suddenly saw one of the two fashion plates coming towards him. He had not paid the slightest attention to these creatures. Their immobility had made him think that they formed an integral part of the setting. He gave a start when the fashion plate stopped in front of him and began to speak. He replied with a selection of insults recited with the earnestness of a lesson well learnt. Out of breath, and faced with the woman's impassive smile, he shrugged his shoulders helplessly. He was not going to be able to get rid of this intruder. To hell with these leeches! And he made a meaningful gesture with his hands. But she was still there. There was nothing left for him to do but capitulate. With a triumphant smile she sat down opposite him and summoned the waiter with a vulgar gesture. She ordered a complicated concoction and drank it with what looked like blissful pleasure.

"Darling," she said a few moments later, "I'm going to put on something livelier. Don't you want to dance, honey?"

Later on, when they were in his room, he became more and more disconcerting. His tousled beard and his jerky movements made him look like a broken-down clockwork puppet. He walked up and down, alternately eloquent and cynical. He waved his arms about to impart a certain rhythm to his words.

"You're probably wondering why I don't look at anything but your belly? All through my childhood I never saw anything but my mother's belly. She didn't buy her dresses at Dior's, and all she wore was a little pagne tied round her waist. I was the last child in a large family— I had thirteen brothers, unless I'm mistaken—and for me my mother's belly was the haven where I took refuge every night, hanging on to the gourds which gave life. That belly warmed me and protected me from the outside world. Today, a woman's belly still has that sort of almost mystic significance for me. The belly, you see, is the seat of a great many social evils such as hunger, cold, fear, unsatisfied desire. You ought to see the bellies of the women in my country! We live in unimaginable poverty, and yet our women have lots of children. It's as if a fellow like me were like a by-product of poverty. Just now, in the bar, you were surprised to see me playing that jazz record over and over again. Why has jazz conquered the world? Because it comes from the very bowels of human

suffering. Look, I'm a Catholic, and even if I don't practice
my religion any more, I sometimes go into a chapel just
to hear religious music. Only, that music was written to
serve as a heaven for uplifted souls. What they need in
church is music that can also express what bodies suffer.
I was reading the other day that in Central Europe some
priests have written scores inspired by jazz, to attract the
young. What does it matter what their aim is? What
interests me is the rehabilitation of Negro music. That's
the stone Christ spoke about which is rejected by the
builders but which becomes the chief cornerstone. Do you
know that in my country, in Africa, black is presented as
the color of sin and evil, and the tom-tom as the instru-
ment of the devil? But everything changes. The tom-tom
has made a noisy entry into the African church. Nobody
insists any more on the curse which was supposed to lie
on the descendants of Ham. From now on, Easter is the
color of an Africa which has succeeded in tipping over
the tombstone under which it was buried."

He stopped to get his breath back, and the woman took
the opportunity to say timidly:

"You talk too much, darling. Come and sit down by
me."

"I don't want the Cross to be the only symbol of
universal suffering," he went on without appearing to take
any notice of the interruption. "Why, look at that, there
on the wall. What is it?"

The woman looked with a stupid expression on her
face, and saw a simple figure in the shape of a hook.

"I can't think what it can be," she stammered.

A snigger answered her.

"Well, well, we belong to the most intelligent race in
the world, and we can't decipher symbols! You're the
only exception then. It's true that we aren't in Africa.
Out there, it's only the Whites who open the gates of
the past. The Negroes can say: 'Open, Sesame' as often
as they like: nothing opens for them. What the Africans

need is to find the magic word themselves which will enable them to move mountains. I would have liked to harness myself to that task, but unfortunately I can't. I've enough to worry about with myself. I'm a bit like that character in Tolstoy who says that he has become his own prison. So you don't know what that picture means? That picture is what I regard as the Cross of the Black world. That kind of hook, in fact, represents a Negro bending his back as a sign of deference or as a sign of suffering under the ill treatment to which he is subjected. Did you know that the black man is descended from india rubber?"

The woman no longer had any doubts. The man was mad. She had only one movement to make to reach the door and get out of the room. But she stayed where she was, unable to make much of all these extraordinary words, yet fascinated by such a flow of language.

"Yes," the Negro went on, "we are descended from india rubber, and our great ancestor, if you like, was Michelin, or rather the fellow you see on the posters advertising that brand of tires. That's why our forefathers and the slaves who were sent to America were able to adapt themselves to a situation that was new to them. Just imagine the deluge which fell on our primitive life for forty days and forty nights, drowning our beliefs and our idols—though only to put others in their place—and washing away everything which made up our world. You might say that the European flood 'whitewashed' our African life away. Why don't you laugh? Don't you think that's funny?"

He was beginning to calm down. It was always like that. Whenever he had one of his inexplicable depressions, he would get drunk first and then look for somebody to serve him as both audience and victim. For the others, the white man in the dock had long since been discharged. For him, the trial had only just begun, and was still going on; and he never missed a chance to pronounce his indictment, as he was doing at this moment.

"A terrible deluge," he went on. "Those who had stayed in the Ark threw themselves into the water to avoid being called savages. All those who were already spinning about, caught in the tumultuous current, were no longer anything but pieces of flotsam. The less they tried to swim against the current, the more they were considered to be civilized. We have your race to thank for that nice little tornado."

"Hey!" protested the young woman. "What are you looking at me like that for? I've never taken any interest in politics, I haven't."

"Oh, because you think that colonization is politics, do you? You're even stupider than I thought. Never mind! Come along with me!"

She followed him passively, and they went into a small room.

"This is my dark room," he explained. "It's here that I develop my photographs. You look surprised, but I'm telling the truth. Thanks to some useful people I know, I do some work as a photographer for a leading paper. But what's the matter with you? You're trembling, honey. Don't tell me you're afraid of Bluebeard?"

"But I'm not trembling."

"Yes, you are. Wait a minute. I'll turn on the light."

The little room, which could not have been swept out for several months, was in a state of incredible disorder. Pieces of paper were strewn about, and there was a basin on the floor. On an old chest of drawers there were a few empty frames and a camera which was still in good condition. An indefinable smell took you by the throat, or rather you could detect a great many different smells in the room. N'Toko hurriedly rummaged about in the chest of drawers and brought out a thick wad of photographs.

"Look at these," he said. "Bluebeard's victims. Count

them if you like. This collection consists of nothing but women—my mistresses, of course. I've got other collections here on lots of other things, but you won't see those. Take a good look at the photos I've given you. That's how I, Bluebeard, kill you—with ridicule. In the colonies you are unbearable with your air of belonging to another planet, but in your own country . . ."

The woman looked, very much against her will, and blushed to the roots of her hair. In each photograph she discovered a more daring posture than in the last. How could these women have agreed to pose in such humiliating ways? It was some time before she came to the end of the collection. Her temples and her heart were pounding. Suddenly she saw nothing more. The room was plunged into darkness and the woman felt huge hands running over her body, like monstrous spiders . . .

"We had a rather stormy scene," Bernard Quillet was saying on the telephone. (Bernard Quillet was the editor of the paper for which N'Toko, to use his own words, "did some work as a photographer.") "In the end he walked out, slamming the door behind him and declaring that I would never see him again. I still haven't got over it. After all, I only sent for him to discuss his job. I told him that with his education it was madness to be satisfied with an irregular post which was badly paid into the bargain. Once again I offered him that post which was waiting for him on the staff of the paper, and which I mentioned to you a year ago, when you recommended the young man to me, saying that he was one of your former students. He rejected the offer and answered me in the most violent terms. The other day, his hotel rang me up to ask me if I had any news of him. Nobody had seen him since the very day we had . . . a few words. I began to feel worried and I even thought of phoning the police. It was then that I remembered you, Professor. You are or at least were his patron to some extent, and perhaps you have some news of him?"

"Alas, no," replied the professor; "but I don't think there's any cause for worry. N'Toko was a whimsical character. You might say that he was an armchair student, who regarded his work as fun. He was pathologically lazy, but he had a phenomenal memory. He was always absolutely unbearable with his air of listening to lectures with only half an ear. All the same, he was never stumped by a question and never failed a written examination. I even got the impression that he came to the university just to while away the time. Until what? I still ask myself that question. He not only had an amazing memory, but also possessed a lively mind. And the two of us fought a great many splendid word-duels. The fellow was intelligent, but terribly disconcerting. A hundred times I thought I had formed a mental picture of his true character. The next day, I always had to admit to myself that the picture was inaccurate. Something had escaped my notice. Today, I still miss the fellow. I must tell you that I haven't seen him since the time when I warmly recommended him to you. It's typical of him to accept such a poor job, purely out of defiance. Yes, out of defiance. He was the *enfant terrible* of the university. He got on the nerves of all his fellow students and his teachers. He hadn't a single friend in the place. He was the most resolutely anti-social animal I have ever known. He didn't play games or go to the students' dances, and he didn't go to the cinema or the theater . . ."

"Do you think, Professor, that this was the behavior of somebody with—how shall I put it?—anti-white sentiments?"

"Not particularly. To tell the truth, that had never occurred to me. Generally speaking, the Africans who come to France can exorcize the devils of colonialism themselves."

"Well, that doesn't get us much further, Professor. I must say I have what you might call forebodings."

"I haven't," declared the professor. "All the same, to

make quite sure, I'll go to see him at his hotel, and I'll keep you informed."

"Good. I'd have done that myself, but we parted on such bad terms . . ."

"I quite understand. In any case I'll tell you how things stand. Good-bye, old chap."

The professor was in his library, a sailor surrounded by a sea of books. From his fifth floor, he had a magnificent view of Paris, and particularly of the Eiffel Tower. Wearing his dressing gown, he was walking up and down, apparently deep in thought. He was smoking nervously, throwing his cigarettes away when they were only three-quarters smoked, and there was an absolute hecatomb of cigarette-ends in the ashtray on his desk.

"Professor," said a timid little voice beside him, "your soup is going to get cold. It's after seven o'clock in the evening."

He had not heard her coming. She belonged, he always thought jokingly, to the cat family. Her behavior revealed a remarkable physical and moral equilibrium. Never a word louder than another, never a movement faster than another. She greeted each new day with an unshakeable serenity. The professor had known this good woman for seventeen years, and during this long period there had been established between them that economy of words and displays of feeling which is to be found only in the case of old married couples and old friends. Yet she was nothing more than his housekeeper. He had engaged her as the result of a newspaper advertisement when he had just lost his wife and needed a servant to look after his flat. He had not remarried since.

"Oh, yes, the soup," said the professor, with an absent minded expression. "It can wait, Madame Bonnet."

After these few words, he started slowly pacing up and down again. A few moments later, he stopped in front of Madame Bonnet and started speaking, though without addressing her in particular—something which did not surprise the good woman, who in any case had ceased to be astonished by anything which happened in this house.

"You see," the professor was saying, "this young fellow lived on nothing but a challenge flung down to himself and to those around him. He wanted to destroy the others, and perhaps in the end he has destroyed himself? Where the devil can he have taken refuge in this big city? I daren't leap to any tragic conclusions, but I can't see him accepting the hospitality of friends."

The professor continued his monologue:

"Yes, I think that that young fellow suffered from persecution mania. Everybody knows that that mania is closely related to insanity. Those who suffer from it are convinced every minute of their lives that people are trying to harm them. Either they take cover behind a shield supposed to protect them against blows which exist only in their imagination, or else fear creates arrows which they shoot off at everybody who approaches them. Let's see, Madame . . ."

These last words were addressed directly to his housekeeper.

"Let's see, Madame. Supposing I went to see you at your home. You are out and I go away, but taking some knickknack with me out of curiosity. Is that theft?"

"That depends, Professor. For you it would be a nondescript knickknack, but for the owner it might be an object of great sentimental value . . ."

"Yes, obviously," said the professor, with a faraway look in his eyes, "this notebook bound in imitation leather which I am holding in my hands may have considerable value for its owner—one of my former pupils, an African. He disappeared from his hotel several days ago. I went to see him the other day, and I used my position as his former tutor to obtain permission to visit his room. That was where I found this little notebook. But I daren't open it yet. It seems to me that man is too quick to open all the doors he sees in front of him. My experience as an old professor makes me rather doubtful whether freedom enlightens the world. On the other hand, there is a case for thinking that curiosity enlightens the world. One of these days, man will open a door through which he won't be able to return. That's the point which I myself have reached. For several days I have been undecided as to whether or not to glance inside this notebook. On the other hand, I tell myself that it may contain some useful clues which would enable me to trace my former pupil."

The professor plunged once again into a silent reverie. Madame Bonnet waited for a moment, then left the room as she had come in, without making the slightest noise.

The professor had the irritating impression that he was about to commit an act of sacrilege, but curiosity and uncertainty were too strong for him. With a hand which was trembling slightly he began turning the pages of his former pupil's private diary. He felt an unconquerable embarrassment as he read date after date followed by a woman's Christian name and the entry: "Submitted to my will." "Will" sometimes became "law," "caprice," or more prosaically, "desire." Only the first three words remained invariable: "Submitted to my . . ."

It was clear that N'Toko led a very busy sex life, but this was of little interest to the professor, who was looking for something else, though he was not sure what. He went through the notebook methodically, reading more dates, more women's Christian names; then, on one page, some writing in a regular script danced before his eyes. His heart missed a beat, and he concentrated his attention on what follows:

N'toko's notebook

I have just arrived in Paris. What activity! What a change from Africa, where it is Time that circles round men who are indifferent out of fatalism or temperament. Here,

*everybody bustles around. Out there, we are condemned—
or we were condemned—like Theseus, to remain in one
place. That won't last. They are busy putting clockwork
inside us, to be able to wind us up and make us move
whenever they wish.*

*Punctuality, the politeness of civilized slaves. I can't see
kings, real kings, putting themselves at its service or being
dependent on it.*

A comparison. *The photograph, the field of vision of
my forefathers. The "advanced" nations: the ambitious
gigantism of the cinema, with its hunger for vast spaces,
vaster than its screens can contain. The photo modestly
frames a backwater. The cinema tries to depict the whole
ocean, though it can't show at the same time the streams
and the rivers which run into that ocean.*

*The finest telescope in the world has only just discovered
a satellite close to the earth, a suburban satellite which is
not thousands of light years distant, but only several
thousand million francs away. Who will be the first astro-
naut to land on that planet?*

*If I were a big noise in the cinema world, what a message
I would give this world! I would make a nonconformist
film, floating out of the zone of gravity of threadbare con-
cepts towards a sort of stratosphere in which time and
space would be abolished. I have always dreamt of this
allegorical film in a hundred different scenes.*

*The first scene would present two characters, one a
photographer, the other a mere lens slavishly obeying the
former. Dialogue. The lens would say: "I am blinded by
the flashes of your camera." The photographer: "That's
inevitable. The aim of my civilization is to blind you.
Then you will wear the spectacles I am making for you."
—"And what if I don't wear them?"—"In that case, you
will be condemned to grope your way in this new world
which I am substituting for yours." Another dialogue. The*

lens: "You have taught me exposures, but you restrict my actions and gestures. Why?"—"I can't trust you yet with the secret of movement. You would escape from my control. For the moment, my law remains unchanged: don't move!"

Tirelessly and implacably, the photographer would go on taking snapshots, progressively stripping the lens of everything it had previously possessed. The lens: "Now I am completely naked."—"That was my aim: to reduce you to such a state of destitution that you can no longer do without me."

The colonization of Africa by the West ought to be prosecuted for rape of a minor. It is not for nothing that that phenomenon is shamelessly referred to as penetration. For posterity, the nineteenth century will be the period in which Europe was swept by a wave of lust. It became a competition to see who could penetrate furthest. Who cared if the victim brutally robbed of her virginity remained marked for the rest of her life? And they call that making history!

The machiavellism and moral ugliness of the Western world! It exports vices to Africa in pretty Pandora's boxes. Those boxes are naturally opened in Africa, and the inhabitants are amazed to see unknown scourges and diseases inexplicably appear.

Look for man here, and you will find only crowds. A terrible insult to God, who is implicitly accused of being nothing but a manufacturer of mass-produced men.

In the beginning, God made the Word. Men, for their part, made the word. These huge rivers of speech displace millions of cubic yards of promises and hopes, but never flow into the ocean of universal happiness. Their Spanish taste for battles of words, in which you keep hearing the same things without the face of the world changing one iota.

In our day, Galileo would say: "The earth revolves all the same," and this "all the same" would be full of meaning. It would mean: yes, but in what direction. Yesterday Africa was the kingdom of H.M. Idler the First, seated on his throne (a chaise-longue). Well, the industrialized West has never had as many idlers (rich men) as it has now. They are prolonging the Idler dynasty on their "relaxing chairs." The West in its turn is moving fast towards the law of minimum effort: reduction of the working week, supremacy of the machine, and so on.

How many ugly sights I have discovered since I arrived in Paris! A comforting thought. The god has fallen off his pedestal. To be sure of that, I must amass evidence. The idea of a film is too fanciful. As for a novel, I very much fear I lack the patience to write one. A book like that has to be written with every-day words, but words capable of destroying the so-called material power of that fallen god. With words charged with a "demystifying" force. Alas, I am afraid of being unable to find such words. But photography would provide the answer. In the absence of a closer reality, I could at least have an accurate copy of this ugly life. I could take masses of photos of all those who have fallen into an abyss. After all, don't the Europeans use the same methods in my country? They never photograph anything but Africa in rags, a grimacing, painted Africa which is more photogenic, it seems.

The ideal: to bring off a composite photograph of this world in all its putrefaction.

I could go back to my country, once my studies were over, and find a high administrative position waiting for me. Instead of that, I have become a turncoat. Why? I think it is because I have never been able to adapt myself to circumstances. This sickly shyness of mine which I have to hide behind a mask of hardness. I am frightened. Am I a monster? I always experience a feeling of unusual ex-

citement and fierce joy every time I photograph a fatal accident. Those awful wounds, that horrible pulp, give me a vague feeling of revenge. It is terrible. Every time that has happened to me, I have had to drown that feeling in a flood of alcohol. There is a Mr. Hyde in me who has Dr. Jekyll completely in his power. There is nothing to be done, and it is impossible to make a move. It is like being in a dark room. I don't know where the door is. Paris is no longer anything but a prison for me and I am my own jailer . . .

The notes stopped there. Then, all of a sudden, light dawned on the professor. The words "I am my own jailer" whirled around in his head in a mad saraband. He realized that N'Toko had not "disappeared" from his room, and that on the contrary he must be there—probably rid for ever of the crushing burden of everything which had weighed upon his short life. A saying by the writer Zweg came back to him: "To try to judge a human being carried away by passion would be as absurd as to call a storm to account or to bring a lawsuit against a volcano."

A MATTER OF TASTE

Alex La Guma

Alex La Guma, who was born in Cape Town in
1925, left South Africa with his family in 1966.
Prior to that time, because of his political activi-
ties, he had been detained by the South African
government, and in 1962 he was placed under house
arrest for five years. La Guma is the author of
And a Threefold Cord (1964), *The Stone Country*
(1967), and *A Walk in the Night and Other Stories*
(1967). "A Matter of Taste" is from the last
volume.

The sun hung well towards the west now so that the
thin clouds above the ragged horizon were rimmed with
bright yellow like the spilt yolk of an egg. Chinaboy stood
up from having blown the fire under the round tin and
said, "She ought to boil now." The tin stood precariously
balanced on two half-bricks and a smooth stone. We had
built the fire carefully in order to brew some coffee and
now watched the water in the tin with the interest of
women at a childbirth.

"There she is," Chinaboy said as the surface broke into
bubbles. He waited for the water to boil up and then
drew a small crushed packet from the side pocket of his
shredded windbreaker, untwisted its mouth and carefully
tapped raw coffee into the tin.

He was a short man with gray-flecked kinky hair, and a
wide, quiet, heavy face that had a look of patience about
it, as if he had grown accustomed to doing things slowly

and carefully and correctly. But his eyes were dark oriental
ovals, restless as a pair of cockroaches.

"We'll let her draw awhile," he advised. He put the
packet away and produced an old rag from another pocket,
wrapped it around a hand and gingerly lifted the tin from
the fire, placing it carefully in the sand near the bricks.

We had just finished a job for the railways and were
camped out a few yards from the embankment and some
distance from the ruins of a onetime siding. The corrugated iron of the office still stood, gaping in places and
covered with rust and cobwebs. Passers had fouled the
roofless interior and the platform was crumbled in places
and overgrown with weeds. The cement curbing still
stood, but cracked and covered with the disintegration
like a welcome notice to a ghost town. Chinaboy got out
the scoured condensed milk tins we used for cups and set
them up. I sat on an old sleeper and waited for the ceremony of pouring the coffee to commence.

It didn't start right then because Chinaboy was crouching with his rag-wrapped hand poised over the can, about
to pick it up, but he wasn't making a move. Just sitting
like that and watching something beyond us.

The portjackson bush and wattle crackled and rustled
behind me and the long shadow of a man fell across the
small clearing. I looked back and up. He had come out
of the plantation and was thin and short and had a pale
white face covered with a fine golden stubble. Dirt lay in
dark lines in the creases around his mouth and under his
eyes and in his neck, and his hair was ragged and thick
and uncut, falling back to his neck and around his temples. He wore an old pair of jeans, faded and dirty and
turned up at the bottoms, and a torn leather coat.

He stood on the edge of the clearing, waiting hesitantly,
glancing from me to Chinaboy, and then back at me. He
ran the back of a grimy hand across his mouth.

Then he said hesitantly: "I smelled the coffee. Hope
you don' min'." Chinaboy said with that quiet careful

smile of his, "Seeing you's here, I reckon I don' min' either." He smiled at me, "you think we can take in a table boarder, pal?"

"Reckon we can spare some of the turkey and green peas."

Chinaboy nodded at the stranger. "Sit, pally. We were just going to have supper."

The white boy grinned a little embarrassedly and came around the sleeper and shoved a rock over with a scarred boot and straddled it. He didn't say anything, but watched as Chinaboy set out another scoured milk tin and lifted the can from the fire and poured the coffee into the cups.

"Help yourself, man. Isn't exactly the mayor's garden party." The boy took his cup carefully and blew at the steam. Chinaboy sipped noisily and said, "Should've had some bake bread. Nothing like a piece of bake bread with cawfee."

"Hot dogs," the white boy said.

"Huh."

"Hot dogs. Hot dogs go with coffee."

"Ooh ja. I heard," Chinaboy grinned. Then he asked: "You going somewhere, Whitey?"

"Cape Town. Maybe get a job on a ship an' make the States."

"Lots of people want to reach the States," I said.

Whitey drank some coffee and said: "Yes, I heard there's plenty of money and plenty to eat."

"Talking about eating," Chinaboy said: "I see a picture in a book, one time. 'Merican Book. This picture was about food over there. A whole mess of fried chicken, mealies—what they call corn—with mushrooms an' gravy, chips, and new green peas. All done up in colors, too."

"Pass me the roast lamb," I said sarcastically.

"Man," Whitey said warming up to the discussion, "Just let me get to something like that and I'll eat till I burst wide open."

Chinaboy swallowed some coffee: "Worked as a waiter

one time when I was a youngster. In one of that big
caffies. You should've seen what all them bastards ate. Just
sitting there shoveling it down. Some French stuff too,
patty grass or something like that."

I said: "Remember the time we went for drunk and
got ten days? We ate mealies and beans till it came out
of our ears!"

Chinaboy said, whimsically: "I'd like to sit down in a
smart caffy one day and eat my way right out of a load
of turkey, roast potatoes, beet salad and angel's food
trifle. With port and cigars at the end."

"Hell," said Whitey, "it's all a matter of taste. Some
people like chicken and othe's eat sheep's heads and
beans!"

"A matter of taste," Chinaboy scowled. "Bull, it's a
matter of money, pal. I worked six months in that caffy
and I never heard nobody order sheep's head and beans!"

"You heard of the fellow who went into one of these
big caffies?" Whitey asked, whirling the last of this coffee
around in the tin cup. "He sits down at a table and takes
out a packet of sandwiches and puts it down. Then he
calls the waiter and orders a glass of water. When the
waiter brings the water, this fellow says: 'Why ain't the
band playing?'"

We chuckled over that and Chinaboy almost choked.
He coughed and spluttered a little and then said, "Another John goes into a caffy and orders sausage and mash.
When the waiter bring him the stuff he take a look and
say: 'My dear man, you've brought me a cracked plate.'
'Hell,' says the waiter. 'That's no crack. That's the
sausage.'"

After we had laughed over that one Chinaboy looked
westward at the sky. The sun was almost down and the
clouds hung like bloodstained rags along the horizon.
There was a breeze stirring the wattle and portjackson,
and far beyond the railway line a dog barked with high
yapping sounds.

Chinaboy said: "There's a empty goods going through here around about seven. We'll help Whitey, here, onto it, so's he can get to Cape Town. Reckon there's still time for some more pork chops and onions." He grinned at Whitey. "Soon's we've had dessert we'll walk down the line a little. There's a bend where it's the best place to jump a train. We'll show you."

He waved elaborately towards me: "Serve the duck, John!"

I poured the last of the coffee into the tin cups. The fire had died to a small heap of embers. Whitey dug in the pocket of his leather coat and found a crumpled pack of cigarettes. There were just three left and he passed them round. We each took one and Chinaboy lifted the twig from the fire and we lighted up.

"Good cigar, this," he said, examining the glowing tip of the cigarette.

When the coffee and cigarettes were finished, the sun had gone down altogether, and all over the land was swept with dark shadows of a purple hue. The silhouetted tops of the wattle and portjackson looked like massed dragons.

We walked along the embankment in the evening, past the ruined siding, the shell of the station-house like a huge desecrated tombstone against the sky. Far off we heard the whistle of a train.

"This is the place," Chinaboy said to Whitey. "It's a long goods and when she takes the turn the engine driver won't see you, and neither the rooker in the guard's van. You got to jump when the engine's out of sight. She'll take the hill slow likely, so you'll have a good chance. Jus' you wait till I say when. Hell, that sound like pouring a drink!" His teeth flashed in the gloom as he grinned. Then Whitey stuck out a hand and Chinaboy shook it, and then I shook it.

"Thanks for supper, boys," Whitey said.

"Come again, anytime," I said, "we'll see we have a tablecloth." We waited in the portjackson growth at the side of the embankment while the goods train wheezed and puffed up the grade, its headlamp cutting a big yellow hole in the dark. We ducked back out of sight as the locomotive went by, hissing and rumbling. The tender followed, then a couple of boxcars, then some coal cars and a flatcar, another boxcar. The locomotive was out of sight.

"Here it is," Chinaboy said, pushing the boy ahead. We stood near the train, hearing it click-clack past. "Take this coal box coming up," Chinaboy instructed. "She's slow. And good luck, pal!"

The coal car came up and Whitey moved out, watching the iron grip on the far end of it. Then as it drew slowly level with him, he reached out, grabbed and hung on, then got a foothold, moving away from us slowly.

We watched him hanging there, reaching for the edge of the car and hauling himself up. Watching the train clicking away, we saw him straddling the edge of the truck, his hand raised in a salute. We raised our hands too.

"Why ain't the band playing? Hell!" Chinaboy said.

THE TAX DODGER

Cameron Duodu

Poet and novelist Cameron Duodu was born in
Ghana in 1937. From 1960 to 1965 he was editor
of the Ghanaian edition of *Drum*, and he has been
for several years the Ghanaian correspondent for
The Observer and director of the Ghana News
Agency. Besides travelling extensively throughout
Europe, Mr. Duodu has spent several months in
the United States, and in 1967 published his first
novel, *The Gab Boys*. "The Tax Dodger" first appeared in *Okyeame*, published by the Ghana Society
of Writers.

I looked round the Court House. I couldn't believe I
was on trial. Why, the court looked much the same as it
did these countless times when I and other boys came to
sit there not because we were interested in how our native
customary law worked but because we got our laughs free
and we loved fun.

I remembered, for instance, that man who had been
brought in for stealing a bag of cocoa. After the prose-
cuting policeman had outlined the case against him, he
was asked to state why he said he was "Not Guilty."

"My Lords, Panel Members, I am an Ewe from Togoland who came to this Golcos to work only last year."

(We laughed at this because a year after Independence,
there he stood still calling Ghana his good old "Golcos.")

"The man who employed me," he went on, "also employed two of his own countrymen. I know their names

and if the court likes, it can ask them whether what I am saying is true or not. One is Yaw Mensah and the other Kwadwo Darko. That Kwadwo Darko is a good man. Whenever he and I meet on our master's cocoa farm, he talks to me nicely as if I belong to his own tribe and asks me whether my dogs have caught any rats. If I say yes, he gives me a shilling and takes some of the rats. Also whenever I get snails, I give them to him for we Ewes don't eat snails like you Twi people."

By this time, we had laughed so much that the illiterate police constable on duty had shouted "WORLER! WORLER!" quite often and even his thick bulldog voice was getting hoarse and beginning to sound a trifle like a girl's treble. Yet, there was no "order" in the courtroom for each time he said "WORLER!" Our laughter was given fresh impetus as he kept on shouting "WORLER!" all the more, not the least bit aware that there was anything wrong with it. And so it went on like a merry-go-round.

The court chairman was a merry old man with a great sense of humor and he didn't worry us much except for an occasional thump he made with his fist on the table. But even he was getting impatient with the man in the dock.

"My friend," he said, "it's all very good of you to tell the court about your friend Kwadwo Darko and his love for snails, or rather, rats!" . . . (laughter) . . . "But I must warn you that the charge against you is a serious one and that you'd better confine yourself to answering it. You mentioned Kwadwo Darko's name only because you said he was one of two people who could bear out what you were going to tell us which you never did. For all I know, you will be telling us next about the way Kwadwo Darko sharpens his cutlass before he goes to his farm . . ." (laughter) . . . "Now, I think it will be a good idea, don't you, if you left your good friend Kwadwo Darko for a bit and told us what you were going to say?"

"Yes, sir!" the man, Yaovi, replied. "I was going to say we do much the same amount of work—myself, Yaw Mensah and Kwadwo Darko. But they get better terms than me; they get the 'abusa' deal by which a third of the gross income that is obtained from the cocoa they tend is given to them. I am only paid a wage of two shillings and sixpence a day, with only a variable bonus to add when the cocoa season comes and my cocoa is sold. So that I can't save as much money as I'd like to save with which to buy a bicycle and go to Togoland . . ."

We really held our sides now. That man must have been a really bush Ewe for no Ewe man who lived in an Akyem town steeped in irrational tribalism such as ours could have lain himself open like that, admitting to a court full of antagonistic Akyem people that a bicycle is one of the most treasured things in Togoland and that if he could get one to take home, he would feel like a Moslem who had been to Mecca! You see, this was a standing joke tribalistic Akyems made at the expense of Ewes and which the latter vehemently refuted.

The man in the dock was quite puzzled by our laughter but went on, not too shaken. "This season, I decided I'd do something to right matters in my favor and when I cut up the fresh cocoa pods, I put some of the beans in a bag and took them to a place away from where I had made my main heap of cocoa beans. But Yaw Mensah saw it and because last time when he asked me for matches, I said I didn't have any and then he saw one drop from my pocket when I was taking out a piece of cola nut to chew, he went and told our master who came and reported me to the police who put handcuffs to my hands . . ."

"But my good friend," said the chairman of the court, "you have as much as admitted the charges against you. Why then do you say you're not guilty?"

"I am not guilty because I wasn't caught by anybody when I was taking the cocoa bag to the place I hid it," the man said, getting heated. "It is the law, isn't it, that when you're caught stealing, they bring you to court? In Togoland, the French people, when they catch you, they beat you with sticks and you are put in chains and if you're not lucky enough, you will even be shot. That's why we have a proverb which says 'It's the fool who allows himself to be caught.' I didn't get caught—it was afterwards that Yaw Mensah went and made 'konkonsa' about me and my master came to the police who put handcuffs to my hands and said I should find somebody to bail me and the Ewe chief-man—there he sits, my Lords—he bailed me . . ."

"COUR-R-R-T RA-A-A-A-I-I-S!" the burly Constable shouted as the chairman got up, followed by the two panel members. They were going to "agyina" to ask the "Old Woman" what she thought of the case. (Who she was nobody knew but whenever the court rose to hold consultation, it was said to be going to ask the "Old Woman" for an opinion. I wondered how much tobacco they bought for her from the fines they got in court). Well, they came back, there was another order for "COUR-R-RT RA-A-A-I-I-S!" and Yaovi got his three months imprisonment and we all went home to see whether our mothers had finished pounding the fruits and vegetables into *fufu* balls.

Yes, I remembered all this as I stood there in the dock and it was quite like a dream—as if I was outside myself and only looking at something that was being acted with me in it.

Even my arrest appeared like a joke—I was going to Kwaa Maanu's store where we boys always gathered, when the OBK (the office bookkeeper in charge of the local authority police station) called me. I was wearing my coffee gabardine trousers which I had sewn in Kumasi some time ago when my grandfather sent me to Ahafo to see about some little cocoa farms he'd got there. I was also wearing brown "talking mokes" to match, a pair of moccasin shoes with a lot of iron protectors at the bottom which were put there not only because I feared the shoes would wear out early but because they made quite a good noise on the hard pavement and that compelled the people to turn round to see who was coming. Yes, I was quite boogied up and when that OBK guy called me, I thought he was going to ask me where I sewed my trousers and where I bought my "mokes" and how much they cost. I had consequently thought up some big figures which would let him know that a guy like me, although "unbeez," that is unemployed, could yet challenge those mouthy working fellows when it came to real good buying. And, of course, I had a lot of big names at the tip of my tongue regarding where I got the trousers made—names that would stagger that bush son-of-a-gun who called himself OBK—"Tiger Bay" for instance—I was sure he'd never heard the name of that famous Kumasi tailoring shop.

You can see my great surprise therefore when he asked me quite bluntly as soon as I got where he was standing: "Have you paid your Land Poll?"

"Land Poll?" I asked in complete bewilderment. I knew it was the basic rate that was levied in most towns and villages but I'd never thought of it in connection with me. Why, Land Poll was paid by grown-ups. I left Middle School only two years ago and although I had a small goatee which gave me quite a dignified look, I never ever thought of myself as a person liable to pay levy.

"Land Poll?" I asked the OBK again, hoping I had not heard him right. He nodded his head and I became convinced that the guy had gone crackers.

"Ho!" I said, "but I'm only a kid you know—I've never paid Land Poll before—I left school only two years ago—I'm unemployed and just about being apprenticed to Tailor Asiedu! Ho! I think you're mistaken—I don't think I'm liable to pay Land Poll. After all, I'm only a kid, you know—just a kid—"

As I said this, I involuntarily ran my hand over the flat top of my "Abidjan" haircut and stroked the thousand and one clusters of hair that passed for my goatee. Perhaps that was against me for the OBK's next statement wasn't reassuring at all.

"You're a kid, are you?" he said. "I bet if you talk to the chief's wife three times, she will have a baby with a monkey face like yours, eh, kid boy? Ho! Ho! You sure aren't gonna get away with any of that crybaby talk. You're gonna pay this levy, man, and I'm gonna see that you do so rightaway!"

He blew his whistle and two stalwarts quickly came out of the chief's place (which served as the courthouse and police station). I recognized one of the stalwarts as the chap who said "WORLER! WORLER!" in court all the time and into whose hands I had always thought it wouldn't be a nice thing at all for anybody to fall. There they came running—two stalwart Northern Ghana Police Constables, ready to do anything their OBK master said.

Guys like me knew those illiterate policemen too well. When they come to you, they don't fool around; they just say: "Massa say, me plus you, come. You go-go or you no go-go?" And with that, they brandish their truncheons and if you are silly enough to argue with them, then God have mercy on you. Their language only extends to as far as "Massa say . . ." Whatever else anybody says is immaterial.

"Issa! Braimah!" the OBK called to them. "Dis boy here, ino pay Lampoll; make you bring am for office!" He walked off and the two stalwarts held me, one by each arm, and marched me to the OBK's office. Within the twinkling of an eye, he had written out a summons against me, asking me to come to court that very day to show cause why I hadn't paid my basic rate. Fortunately, he didn't ask me to find somebody to offer me bail and I strode out of the office, with only the piece of paper he'd given me to remind me of the morning's unpleasant experience.

It was eight-thirty when the OBK caught me—the time we boys usually boogied up to come to town. I was due in court at two o'clock. Well, I got to Kwaa Maanu's store and, as usual, the whole pack of lads was there. There they all sat in the bar adjoining the store, each with an empty bottle and glass beside him. You see, Maanu's store-owner was an avaricious old bird who objected to our collecting up there like that and taking things easy without buying anything, and in the past, whenever he came to find us there, he'd drive us out. But Kwaa Maanu was a good pal—the long hours he sat alone at the store had made him appreciative of good company and he bought the idea that we should have empty bottles by our sides whilst sitting there. When the store-owner came, he would be floored for he would have no way of proving that it was not we who actually bought the beer from the empty bottles that stood in front of us. Kwaa Maanu would swear by us at all costs, damn his master. So there we always sat, carefree and absolutely uninhibited—talking about anything from the latest attempts on the moon to the latest pranks on Oto, the *dekyee* (meat seller) who had gone haywire.

As soon as I took my seat at the table in the centre of the bar, I put my hand in my hip-pocket and took out the summons the OBK had given me, thinking I'd rock the place with this bit of hot news. As soon as they saw it, however, they all chanted in unison: "Yieeeeeeee! Pall Mall! Pall Mall!"

I knew too well what "Pall Mall" meant in our parlance. We discovered the name from the game of "Monopoly" and liked the sound of it and since "Pall" sounded like "Pour" (to us at any rate) and "Mall" like "More," we applied it whenever we wanted to say that more had been added or "poured in." For instance, if we were playing cards and somebody brought forward a spade, he'd say "Pall Mall! Pall Mall." Words like this made us quite unintelligible to the elder folks of the village but it was those which made us clique together as a bunch.

Well, the boys greeted my summons sheet with "Pall Mall! Pall Mall" and very soon each of them was bringing a similar thing out of his pocket. They were all assembled on top of the table—a good pack of pink paper they were, I assure you, and we all burst out laughing and kicked chairs and tossed the papers about. Then, the boys gave me the lowdown. They had all been dealt with in exactly the same manner as myself. First, the friendly call from the OBK, the moment of suspense and then there was the Land Poll thrust at them followed by the two stalwart constables.

We all agreed it had been a deft move on the part of the OBK but wondered how it all got into his damned thick socket of a head in the first place. Many suggestions were put forward—and one was that he had "chopped" some of the Local Council's money and wanted to save himself from exposure and a possible prison sentence by arresting people for not paying Land Poll and getting the court to fine them. There were many suggestions like that but it was what Yaw Kyere said which went properly into everybody's ears.

"Friends, Ghanaians, Countrymen!" he said, in his usual imitation of Mark Anthony. We all knew that was the only bit of Anthony's speech he remembered from his Oxford English Reader Book Six but we let it pass and never molested him for assuming literary airs.

"Friends, Ghanaians, Countrymen," he said. "The plain fact is we Gab Boys are out of favour in town. Last time when I was passing one of the palm-wine bars, I heard some of the grown-ups discussing us. They said: 'These boys are getting too many on our streets—they're finished school and yet won't go out of town to look for work and are staying here, not caring to go to farm with

their parents to help produce more food. They're just a
hell of a nuisance, they are; and if nothing is done about
them, they're going to become a breed of lawless wild
ones who will just terrorize this peaceful village of ours.' "

There were angry cries of protest at this from all the
boys; for although we liked dressing like cowboys and
occasionally yelled across the streets in Injun style, halting
oncoming traffic, that was only to attract attention from
the dames and was nothing more than a superficial display
of tough guy prowess.

"I challenged them on this," Yaw Kyere hastily assured
us, "and pointed out that although it was true we all
dressed in *tunaabo* (gun-mouth) or drain-pipe trousers
and occasionally put on jeans and broad-brim hats, that
was only an outward show. Inside, deep down, I added,
we were sweeter than angels, true, true! Well, those
grown-up fellows, they looked at me and laughed. 'Sweeter
than angels, eh?' Agya Toroh said." (Agya Toroh's real
name was Kwame Kaakyire but because he was fond of
saying things which people didn't want said about them,
we all called him "Agya Toroh," meaning something like
"Father of Lies.")

"Yes, Agya Toroh challenged my statement that we
were sweeter than angels and cited the 'Brokages Case' to
prove that we weren't anything of the sort."

"Yie-e-e-e! B-r-o-o-o-k-a-g-e-s! B-r-o-o-o-k-e!" . . . all
the boys shouted when Yaw Kyere mentioned this case. It
happened only last Christmas. An Akuapem man called
Yaw Boafo had a beer store just a few yards from where
our "bench" Kwaa Maanu had his, and was fond of
attracting customers who would otherwise have bought
from our pal, thus depriving him of quite a lot of com-
mission. We all resented this for we didn't like strangers
to make money in our town though we all wanted to
travel somewhere to make money. Anyway this Yaw
Boafo was a fool for he kept his empty bottles uncovered
at the back of his store where we usually sat with our

dames on a *bonhon* (iron pipe) which I think was once meant to serve as a drain for one of the bridges in our village but was thought better of and so left there for us. There were quite a number of stones near this *bonhon* and occasionally a lad would pick one and hurl it into the heap of bottles: "T-o-o-o-o-o-oh-h." We loved that "t-o-o-o-h-h" sound, man, and we would do it for no reason than just to hear it sound.

Yaw Boafo would come out of his shop and rain abuses on us whenever "T-o-o-o-o-h-h!" sounded. But we would hurl his insults back at him and since he was only one and we were many, he got the worse part of it and we weren't bothered and went on making "T-o-o-o-o-h-h! . . . T-o-o-o-o-o-h-h" occasionally, as our mood dictated. However, since this was spasmodic, quite a lot of bottles remained for Yaw Boafo. But on Twenty-fourth Night, we thought better of our occasional job and decided we'd bombard the whole lot of bottles and peradventure, force Yaw Boafo out of competition with our pal, Kwaa Maanu. So after going round the town firing toy guns and shouting and burning the sheds of the market women (all these were accepted practice in our village, you know; the market woman whose table or shed was burnt would be blamed by the others for not having enough foresight to hide her things in a safe place on Twenty-fourth Night. No blame was attached to us at all. You see, the people in our village were very liberal and they knew without being told that boys will be boys and must needs have their fun, damn whoever suffered as a result)—yeah, after we'd fired guns and made bonfires and whooped across the streets and fought with one another and drunk a hell lot of *akpeteshie* (local gin), we all came back to the *bonhon*. One of our most "tired" boys, that is, one of those who knew the world most, "Mark Brown"—the "African Cowboy"—took a chalk and wrote in big block letters on top of the heap of bottles: "EASY BOTTLES, EASY BROKE!"

Well, Mark wrote that in white block letters on the black wall against which the bottles were heaped and as the last of the gang converged on the *bonhon*, they all filled their pockets with stones, ready to go into action the moment word was given. We sat on the *bonhon* for a while harassing the few girls who were about and then when Mark thought he had had enough black looks from the girls, he went and stood a little way up front and putting his hands to his lips in true Tarzan style, yelled: "CHA-A-A-R-R-GE!"

Before his words had died down his throat, hundreds of stones were hurtling into the heap of bottles "T-o-o-o-o-o-h-h! To-o-o-o-o-h! To-o-o-o-h-h!"

Just as the last stone was hitting the last of the thousand or so bottles, up showed Yaw Boafo, wearing only a pair of shorts and his eyes flashing wild with anger. He came with one of his best friends in town, a chap called Yaw Ampoma—also dressed in shorts which was strange for he was one of the holders of traditional office in the town. But it wasn't too surprising because we believed he was a fool and he was always broke, though he was called with the prefix, Opanin (elder), in respect for his office. He liked to befriend strangers for he managed to get loans from them, ignorant as they were of his always-broke condition and his record of unpaid loans. Maybe they were deceived by his title—they were flattered to have an "elder" of the town as a friend. He, for his part, always took care to get people to address him with the title Opanin whenever he was walking with strangers.

Well, this man and Yaw Boafo were close friends because Yaw Boafo gave him both loans and free palm wine and even an occasional beer. As soon as they got to us, the "elder" shouted out: "Remain where you are, all of you. I have seen you all." And he began to call out our names while Yaw Boafo wrote them down or pretended to do so—we had heard he was illiterate but he had pencil and paper all the same. The while, we stood silent like some dangerous beasts who were being harried but who had not yet made up their minds how to strike back.

Circumstances decided our course of action for us. One of our toughest guys, Kwasi Fori, was standing a little away from us, passing water against a wall. Opanin Yaw Ampoma could not see him properly from where he stood and went towards him saying: "You big coward! You think you can fool us by that eh?—pissing unconcernedly as if you were not one of the criminals! Turn round and let me see your wicked face!" With that, he wheeled Kwasi Fori round, causing urine to spill all over his brand new gabardine trousers.

Kwasi Fori eyed him coolly from the corners of his eyes, just as Roy Rogers does when somebody handles Trigger roughly. Opanin Ampoma wasn't perturbed at all for he was a tall and burly fellow with strong arms and a big chest while Kwasi Fori was small and only measured up to the nape of Opanin Ampoma's neck. "He is called Kwasi Fori; his father is Kwaku Antwi, the chief's linguist's brother!" Opanin Ampoma shouted out to his friend Yaw Boafo.

In the meantime, Kwasi had buttoned up his trousers again coolly, and just as Opanin Ampoma's words died down and he was retracing his steps back to where Yaw Boafo stood, Kwasi let him have it—just where we knew he'd do it—right up in the middle of his protruding palm wine fattened belly. Opanin Ampoma bent forward, screaming: "Agye-e-e-e-eh! Waku me!" (My father! He's killed me!) As he bent his huge frame forward, clutching his stomach with both hands, Kwasi went into action again and gave him two terrific socks on the jaw—wham! wham! while we yelled in unison that Ga cry of applause at blows which we had learnt from the cinema halls of Accra and which is unprintable.

The three blows following quickly upon each other were all that was needed to transform Opanin Ampoma into a huge piece of beef ready to be pounded into pulp by the obliging fists of Kwasi Fori. "Wham! Wham! Wham! puh! wham! puh! wham!" it went. And we yelled that Ga cry each time a blow sounded so that it looked exactly as if we were actually at a cowboy film and were watching the screen hero giving the villain the works. At one stage, Opanin Ampoma's "Agyeeeeee-h Agyeeeeeeee-h" could have been heard for a mile afield. Finally, he hit upon a strategy—he thought if he fell, and pretended to be unconscious, Kwasi Fori's deluge of blows would cease. So as Kwasi caught him one more in the jaw, he fell forward, limp. He did not of course know that Kwasi didn't spend his time at the cinemas dozing. Kwasi let him fall halfway and then caught him back by his belt and wheeled him round suddenly, his left hand ready to smack home one more time. It never did. Yaw Boafo had seen too much and had at last forgotten his own fear and ran up to hold Kwasi's drawn left hand to prevent him from giving any further punishment to his "elder" friend. We closed in as soon as Yaw Boafo held Kwasi's hand. But he spoke quickly before we could do him anything.

"My friends, I beg your pardon—I won't take any notice of the broken bottles—please let my friend and me go free!"

"WHAT ABOUT MY GAB TROUSERS?" Kwasi Fori asked, a dangerous glint in his eyes. He added force to his words by rounding his fists as if ready to hit again that moment.

"Oh—I'll p-pay back its p-price for you! How much is it?"

"The material cost four guineas and the tailor charged one quid—five pounds four in all! Let it make me wa-a-a-a-h! right now!"

Yaw Boafo put his hand to his pocket. He pulled out five pounds. "Please take this—that's all I have at the moment," he said.

Kwasi took the money and then began to walk away towards his house. We all followed him. But Opanin

Ampoma had now found better use of his tongue than merely saying "AGYEEEEEEEEI!" with it and shouted back at us "What about the trousers? If you h-h-have t-t-taken the money, then b-b-bring the trousers to him?"

One of Kwasi Fori's qualities we liked best was his never failing sense of humor. He always had the right word to say at the right time to make everybody laugh. He said to Opanin Ampoma: "If you are a man, come here and pull the trousers off me!" And he said it without the slightest trace of a laugh in his voice which made it all the more funny for us and we all burst out laughing. Yaw Boafo consoled his friend and said: "Let him take it —what do you want with a pair of ruined trousers?"

We followed Kwasi to his house where he took one of the pound notes Yaw Boafo had given him and sent three of the smaller boys to go with it to buy eight tins of corned beef. While we waited, we discussed the fight and praised Kwasi, saying that not even Burt Lancaster of "Ten Tall Men" fame could have done it better. We all laughed again when somebody said he wondered whether Opanin Ampoma would dare take the case to the Police Station. We knew he could do no such thing for if the other "elders" of the chief heard he had been beaten up by a "commoner," they would ask him to slaughter a sheep to pacify his ancestors who had thus been vilified and we knew his pocket and the price of a sheep did not meet by a long mile. He would keep mum—the worst he could say when inquisitive people asked about his swollen lips and face would be that he had been stung by *mpenoa* (wasps) which he encountered when he went to see whether his cola nuts had begun to ripen. He wasn't above that kind of lie.

The corned beef did not take long to come and we ate up all the eight tins raw, that is without adding any food. By the time we finished, a few of us had cuts where the tins had bruised the backs of our hands—nobody had enough patience to wait until the contents were emptied into a pan or plate. We struggled over it and when we'd eaten it all up, we drank some water from a barrel that was nearby. Then we each went to his home to sleep peacefully. We were happy to be alive—such adventure as the one we had been through made life worth living.

You see, to be quite frank, we had nothing to live for. We respected nothing and nobody and no one respected us, no one cared two hooks about us. There we were, none older than twenty, a whole pack of us, our imagination fuelled to combustion point by the many action-packed American films we saw each time we took a trip to a big town. And yet we had no creative occupation to keep us busy and away from mischief. We had all finished school, and yet we had no work. With us, you finished school when you reached Middle Form Four—Standard Seven. Those who were clever would go on to secondary schools after successfully taking the Common Entrance Examination. None of us had even bothered to take that exam when it came to our turn—two turns each of us had—one in standard five and one in standard six. And each time, those of us who could get their parents to give them money took it and travelled outside the town to some place and chopped it. For we knew we didn't stand a dog's chance. Imagine all the Standard Five and Standard Six children in the whole country fighting for the few places in the extremely few Government assisted secondary schools and technical schools. Soaaaaaaaaaaa! We wouldn't even try. As for the encouraged secondary schools that held their own entrance examinations, you didn't need to worry about them. If you had the money, somehow you would find admission into one, damn entrance exams. It was the dough that counted. You could depend on their headmasters to take in as many students as possible and give them as few qualified teachers as possible. It was a business and we knew it. Our parents had no money anyway. And even if they had, we knew of many young chaps who had gone to such secondary schools and failed even to get grade five at the school certificate examination. They came home and tried to sit for the exam as private candidates. But they failed again and again and became a liability to their parents. Even if they succeeded in getting work, because they did not have their school certificate they got very poor pay, just slightly better than what we Standard Seven lads would get if we found jobs.

We knew all about these things and so we were not too bothered about our lack of education. If we had no work, it was not because we were bad but because there were no jobs. Tell us to go to farm—to "go back to the land" —and we would say: "Look here, sir! If we wanted to be farmers we would not have wasted a full ten years learning to read and write. If we wanted to be farmers like our fathers, we would not have gone to school to get whipped and driven about and bullied and taught simple interest and other sums which made our heads reel. No, sir. If we are to be farmers at all, we don't want to just weed a piece of land and plant yam or plantain or cocoyam or just cassavas or vegetables on it, the topsy-turvy way we've seen our fathers do for years and years. The subsistence farming which barely gives them enough food to live on and keeps them for ever at the mercy of moneylenders. No, sir. If we wanted that kind of thing, we wouldn't have got our fathers to scrape their last pennies to pay our school fees and buy our fantastically expensive text-books."

In fact, our fathers would be annoyed if we suggested that we should follow their footsteps and become farmers. A farmer who was illiterate sent his son to school not only to get him to write the occasional letter he might wish to send or to read the one which he received. After all, there were letter writers, professional ones, who would be glad to oblige in the unlikely event of the farmer wishing to communicate with anyone outside his small world.

No, your father sent you to school to become a clerk who wore a white shirt whom he could show off as *me ba*

krakyenii no (my educated son). If he wanted you to
become a farmer like himself, he would not have paid
your fees for a good ten years and bought you a school
uniform every year in the bargain. He would just have
started you off when you were a kid and gone to his farm
with you every day of the week except Sunday. By that,
he would not have got you to become a farmer but to
help produce food instead of just eating it and whittling
away the little money that cocoa brought. No, sir. His
son was educated so that he could come home from a big
town occasionally overburdened with cakes and Nsawam
bread and a good swell city hat or pipe for grand old pap.
Or that he should send an occasional money order home
and get his illiterate father to go round all the educated
people in the village to have them read the correct sum
on it for him and show him how he could let the piece
of paper become money which could buy real tobacco.
Yes, sir. Such was the purpose of educating his son. He
should wear a white shirt and gabardine trousers and
"talking" shoes and a nice wristwatch and get people to
look at him whenever he walked in the streets. He wanted
people to say: "That is the son of Agya (a prefix used for
all elderly males) so-and-so!"

Well, we had no jobs and were highly imaginative.
Thank God, food was no problem once we stayed in our
town. Ever since creation, no Akyem-born lad living in
his own village had ever starved, no matter what kind of
guy he was. Let him drink *akpeteshie* every day and come
home to rain abuses on his mother; he would still get his
round ball of *fufu* in the evening. Let him roam the
streets breaking people's bottles and filling up the space
in people's bars. When he got home, his old mother
would have come back from her farm and would have
somehow managed to pound her *fufu* single-handed and
his sizeable ball would be there waiting. If the meat in
the soup was small, who cared? As Mark Brown would
say, "A BEGGAR HAS NO CHOOSE." The proverb in

Twi was *Su kon no nnsu nam* (Cry for food and not for meat).

"So, what do you think we should do?" Yaw Kyere asked the palm-wine drinkers when he found their arguments too strong. (He wasn't a Mark Anthony for nothing. He always knew that people could criticize hell out of you but when you passed the buck on to them and asked them to suggest concrete ways by which you could improve the matters they so well disliked, they always fell flat on their backs.) "What do you think we should do?" Yaw Kyere asked them.

One said: "Of course you should all be rounded up and sent to the Borstal Institutes. When you eat kenkey and dried fish for three years, you will have some sense knocked into your empty skulls."

"But would there be enough Borstal Institutes to accommodate all of us?" Yaw Kyere asked. "Don't forget," he pointed out, "that we are not the only boys of our type in this country. We are Esiaho boys. Okay. There are Kibi boys; Apedwa boys; Accra boys; Kumasi boys; Sakasaka boys . . . And also girls!"

The fellows up there were staggered. They had always thought of us in a vacuum; they didn't realize that we were only a branch of a whole lot of unproductive young worth-nothings who were plaguing themselves and the country.

So Yaw Kyere kicked some of the wind out of those palm-wine drinkers but he didn't stop them feeling resentful about us. He said as he left the place, he heard them talking hu-hu-hu-hu about us. And not very long afterwards he saw the OBK go in there for his afternoon calabash of palm wine. So it was quite possible that the Land Poll business came into his head after he had heard all the things those palm-wine people said about us. In fact, it could have been suggested to him by them for they themselves were unproductive; most of them thrived on little cocoa farms left to them by their dead uncles and since the cocoa season comes only twice a year, they loafed about like us most of the time, taking odd farming jobs that came to them, *dakoro-adwuma* (one-day jobs). We were becoming a threat to them, so they figured; though in what respect I don't understand. They therefore boozed up the OBK and got him to start the Land Poll campaign against us. They were talking like that when Opanin Yaw Ampoma, the principal victim of the "Brokages Incident," entered. As soon as he heard what they were talking about, he supported the idea that if the OBK got us all rounded up and brought us to court for not paying our Land Poll, some of our arrogance would vanish. Of course, he would see that we got the kind of justice we deserved—even if he himself, as an elder, wasn't on the local court panel the day we went to court, he would see the fellows who would be on it and get to them the threat we were to the whole village, and so understand and give us something hot to take the wind out of us. All this, of course, was Yaw Kyere's theory. And like the good Anthony that he was, he warned us that it would be dangerous, in spite of what we had been told, to ignore the summons on the ground that it was corrupt. If we refused to go to court, he warned, that would bring warrants against us and, as everybody knew, a warrant was a much stronger thing than a summons. And infinitely more trouble-causing. They were always accompanied by handcuffs.

But talk of warrants had just the opposite effect on us boys. "Let them bring the darn things," we said. "We won't go to court, let them bring the warrants."

I regret to say I was the only one who came out against the idea of not going to court. It wasn't that I was afraid of the warrant (though it was quite frightening to think of it—a warrant!) but I thought we had a good case. Every court in the world would acquit us, I argued. For where on earth were people arrested for not paying taxes when they were known to be unemployed? Moreover, we were minors; all of us were still in our teens, even if we were late there; and we left school only two years ago and although we had some hairs on our chins, that didn't mean we were grown-up. In our society, being grown-up was a status which came to you. When you left school and got work to do and earned some money you became grown-up. But not before. We could get the court to understand that, I was sure.

"And also, we do not vote!" said Mark Anthony.

"YE-E-E-E-E-S-S-S!!!   EXA-A-A-C-T-LY!!   W-E D-O-N-'T   V-O-O-OTE," we all said in our usual unison.

"Now you see we have an even better argument," I said. "People who pay taxes are those who vote. We don't yet have the vote so we can't be expected to pay taxes. Remember what we learnt during history lessons?" I asked with a sudden touch of genius. "The American revolution was partly caused by taxation without representation."

In spite of this sound defence I thought we'd got, however, the other lads still maintained that they would not go to court and present it. They said the only thing that could make a local authority court see sense was a showdown. When you challenged its authority, then it would begin to see the arguments in your favor. But if you succumbed to its call and put yourself in its hands, then woe unto you.

I was still not convinced and they rained abuses on me, calling me "a girl in boy's clothing" and many other such unsavory names. As for my reference to the American Revolution, it was brushed aside, one clever lad pointing out that that happened in 1666(!)—long ago—and anyway it was against a British Queen! Whereas we no more had a British Queen but our own Osagyefo. I was beaten flat for I never remember the dates of historical facts and as soon as somebody argues against me and quotes a date, I just keep quiet. All the same, I said

I would go to court and argue my case properly and show the court that we young boys, too, knew the law. What could they say to the argument that we didn't vote? Or that we didn't work?

Hence it was that I stood in the dock that two o'clock. My mother had just returned from her farm and was sitting with the crowd, still in her farm clothes. I wondered what went on inside her mind! Did she think I was an ass? I had heard the other women there whispering that I was too *mfenim*, that is I was "too known." I thought I knew better than anybody else. Where were the other boys who had got summonses like myself? They were on the streets playing and here was I, showing all the world that I was a brave and wise lad who was not afraid to go to court. Well, let me wait and see.

⦿

A Meeting in the Dark

James Ngugi

James Ngugi is clearly the most important contemporary writer from East Africa. He was born in
Kenya and studied at Alliance High School and
later at Makerere University College, Uganda. He
is the author of three novels—*Weep Not, Child*
(1964), *The River Between* (1965), and *A Grain
of Wheat* (1967)—and one drama, *The Black Her-
mit* (1968). Most recently, Mr. Ngugi has been
teaching English at Makerere University College.

His mother used to tell him stories. "Once upon a time
there was a young girl who lived with her father and
mother in a lonely house that was hidden by a hill. The
house was old but strong. When the rains came and the
winds blew, the house remained firm. Her father and
mother liked her, but they quarreled sometimes and she
would cry. Otherwise, she was happy. Nobody knew of
the house. So nobody came to see them. Then one day a
stranger came. He was tall and handsome. He had milk-
white teeth. Her mother gave him food. Then he told them
of a beautiful country beyond the hill. The girl wanted to
go there. Secretly, she followed the man. They had not
gone very far when the stranger turned into an Irimu. He
became ugly and he had another mouth at the back which
was hidden by his long hair. Occasionally, the hair was
blown by the wind. Flies were taken in and the mouth

would be shut. The girl ran back. The bad Irimu followed her. She ran hard, hard, and the Irimu could not catch her. But he was getting nearer her all the time. When she came close to her home, she found the Irimu had stopped running. But the house was no longer there. She had no home to go to and she could not go forward to the beautiful land, to see all the good things, because the Irimu was on the way."

How did the story end? John wondered. He thought: "I wish I were young again in our old home, then I would ask my mother about it." But now he was not young; not young any more. And he was not a man yet!

He stood at the door of the hut and saw his old, frail but energetic father coming along the village street, with a rather dirty bag made out of strong calico swinging by his side. His father always carried this bag. John knew what it contained: a Bible, a hymn book, and probably a notebook and a pen. His father was a preacher. It must have been he who had stopped his mother from telling him stories. His mother had stopped telling him stories long ago. She would say, "Now, don't ask for any more stories. Your father may come." So he feared his father. John went in and warned his mother of his father's coming. Then his father came in. John stood aside, then walked towards the door. He lingered there doubtfully, then he went out.

"John, hei, John!"

"Baba!"

"Come back."

He stood doubtfully in front of his father. His heart beat faster and an agitated voice within him seemed to ask: Does he know?

"Sit down. Where are you going?"

"For a walk, father," he answered evasively.

"To the village?"

"Well—yes—no. I mean nowhere in particular." John saw his father look at him hard, seeming to read his face.

John sighed a very slow sigh. He did not like the way his father eyed him. He always looked at him as though John was a sinner, one who had to be watched all the time. "I am," his heart told him. John guiltily refused to meet the old man's gaze and looked past him and appealingly to his mother who was quietly peeling potatoes. But she seemed to be oblivious of everything around her.

"Why do you look away? What have you done?"

John shrank within himself with fear. But his face remained expressionless. However, he could hear the loud beats of his heart. It was like an engine pumping water. He felt no doubt his father knew all about it. He thought: "Why does he torture me? Why does he not at once say he knows?" Then another voice told him: "No, he doesn't know, otherwise he would have already jumped at you." A consolation. He faced his thoughtful father with courage.

"When is the journey?"

Again John thought—why does he ask? I have told him many times. Aloud, he said,

"Next week, Tuesday."

"Right. Tomorrow we go to the shops, hear?"

"Yes, Father."

"Then be prepared."

"Yes, Father."

"You can go."

"Thank you, Father." He began to move.

"John!"

"Yes?" John's heart almost stopped beating. That second, before his father's next words, was an age.

"You seem to be in hurry. I don't want to hear of you loitering in the village. I know you young men, going to show off just because you are going away! I don't want to hear of trouble in the village."

Much relieved, he went out. He could guess what his father meant by not wanting trouble in the village. How did the story end? Funny, but he could not remember how his mother had ended it. It had been so long ago. Her home was not there. Where did she go? What did she do?

"Why do you persecute the boy so much?" Susan spoke for the first time. Apparently she had carefully listened to the whole drama without a word. Now was her time to speak. She looked at her tough old preacher who had been a companion for life. She had married him a long time ago. She could not tell the number of years. They had been happy. Then the man became a convert. And everything in the home put on a religious tone. He even made her stop telling stories to the child. "Tell him of Jesus. Jesus died for you. Jesus died for the child. He must know the Lord." She too had been converted. But she was never blind to the moral torture he inflicted on the boy (that's what she always called John), so that the boy had grown up mortally afraid of him. She always wondered if it was love for the son. Or could it be a resentment because, well, they two had "sinned" before marriage? John had been the result of that sin. But that had not been John's fault. It was the boy who ought to complain. She often wondered if the boy had . . . but no. The boy had been very small when they left Fort Hall. She looked at her husband. He remained mute, though his left hand did, rather irritably, feel about his face.

"It is as if he was not your son. Or do you . . ."

"Hm, sister." The voice was pleading. She was seeking a quarrel but he did not feel equal to one. Really, women could never understand. Women were women, whether saved or not. Their son had to be protected against all evil influences. He must be made to grow in the footsteps of the Lord. He looked at her, frowning a little. She had made him sin but that had been a long time ago. And he had been saved. John must not follow the same road.

"You ought to tell us to leave. You know I can go away. Go back to Fort Hall. And then everybody . . ."

"Look, sister." He hastily interrupted. He always called

her sister. Sister-in-the-Lord, in full. But he sometimes wondered if she had been truly saved. In his heart, he prayed: Lord, be with our sister Susan. Aloud, he continued, "You know I want the boy to grow in the Lord."

"But you torture him so! You make him fear you!"

"Why! He should not fear me. I have really nothing against him."

"It is you. You. You have always been cruel to him . . ." She stood up. The peelings dropped from her frock and fell in a heap on the floor.

"Stanley!"

"Sister." He was startled by the vehemence in her voice. He had never seen her like this. Lord, take the devil out of her. Save her this minute. She did not say what she wanted to say. Stanley looked away from her. It was a surprise, but it seemed he feared his wife. If you had told people in the village about this, they would not have believed you. He took his Bible and began to read. On Sunday he would preach to a congregation of brethren and sisters.

Susan, a rather tall, thin woman, who had once been beautiful, sat down again and went on with her work. She did not know what was troubling her son. Was it the coming journey?

Outside, John strolled aimlessly along the path that led from his home. He stood near the wattle tree which was a little way from his father's house, and surveyed the whole village. They lay before his eyes—crammed—rows and rows of mud and grass huts, ending in sharp sticks that pointed to heaven. Smoke was coming out of various huts, an indication that many women had already come from the *shambas*. Night would soon fall. To the west, the sun was hurrying home behind the misty hills. Again, John looked at the crammed rows and rows of huts that formed Makeno Village, one of the new mushroom "towns" that grew up all over the country during the Mau Mau war. It looked so ugly. A pang of pain rose in his heart and he felt like crying—I hate you, I hate you. You trapped me alive. Away from you, it would never have happened. He did not shout. He just watched.

A woman was coming towards where he stood. A path into the village was just near there. She was carrying a big load of *kuni* which bent her into an Akamba-bow shape. She greeted him.

"Is it well with you, Njooni?"

"It is well with me, mother." There was no trace of bitterness in his voice. John was by nature polite. Everyone knew of this. He was quite unlike the other proud, educated sons of the tribe—sons who came back from the other side of the waters with white or Negro wives who spoke English. And they behaved just like Europeans! John was a favorite, a model of humility and moral perfection. Everyone knew that though a clergyman's son, John would never betray the tribe.

"When are you going to—to—"

"Makerere?"

"Makelele." She laughed. The way she pronounced the name was funny. And the way she laughed too. She enjoyed it. But John felt hurt. So everyone knew of this.

"Next week."

"I wish you well."

"Thank you, mother."

She said quietly—as if trying to pronounce it better— "Makelele." She laughed at herself again but she was tired. The load was heavy.

"Stay well, son."

"Go well and in peace, mother."

And the woman who all the time had stood, moved on, panting like a donkey, but obviously pleased with John's kindness.

John remained long looking at her. What made such a woman live on day to day, working hard, yet happy? Had she much faith in life? Or was her faith in the tribe?

She and her kind, who had never been touched by ways of the white man, looked as though they had something to cling to. As he watched her disappear, he felt proud that they should think well of him. He felt proud that he had a place in their esteem. And then came the pang. *Father will know. They will know.* He did not know what he feared most; the action his father would take when he knew, or the loss of the little faith the simple villagers had placed in him, when they knew.

He went down to the small local teashop. He met many people who wished him well at the college. All of them knew that the Pastor's son had finished all the white man's learning in Kenya. He would now go to Uganda; they had read this in the *Baraza*, a Swahili weekly paper. John did not stay long at the shop. The sun had already gone to rest and now darkness was coming. The evening meal was ready. His tough father was still at the table reading his Bible. He did not look up when John entered. Strange silence settled in the hut.

"You look unhappy." His mother first broke the silence. John laughed. It was a nervous little laugh.

"No, mother," he hastily replied, nervously looking at his father. He secretly hoped that Wamuhu had not blabbed.

"Then I am glad."

She did not know. He ate his dinner and went out to his hut. A man's hut. Every young man had his own hut. John was never allowed to bring any girl visitor in there. He did not want "trouble." Even to be seen standing with one was a crime. His father could easily thrash him. He wished he had rebelled earlier like all the other young educated men. He lit the lantern. He took it in his hand. The yellow light flickered dangerously and then went out. He knew his hands were shaking. He lit it again and hurriedly took his big coat and a huge *Kofia* which were lying on the unmade bed. He left the lantern burning, so that his father would see it and think him in. John bit his lower lip spitefully. He hated himself for being so girlish. It was unnatural for a boy of his age.

Like a shadow, he stealthily crossed the courtyard and went on to the village street.

He met young men and women, lining the streets. They were laughing, talking, whispering. They were obviously enjoying themselves. John thought, they are more free than I am. He envied their exuberance. They clearly stood outside or above the strict morality that the educated ones had to be judged by. Would he have gladly changed places with them? He wondered. At last, he came to the hut. It stood at the very heart of the village. How well he knew it—to his sorrow. He wondered what he would do! Wait for her outside? What if her mother came out instead? He decided to enter.

"*Hodi!*"

"Enter. We are in."

John pulled down his hat before he entered. Indeed they were all there—all except she whom he wanted. The fire in the hearth was dying. Only a small flame from a lighted lantern vaguely illuminated the whole hut. The flame and the giant shadow created on the wall seemed to be mocking him. He prayed that Wamuhu's parents would not recognize him. He tried to be "thin," and to disguise his voice as he greeted them. They recognized him and made themselves busy on his account. To be visited by such an educated one who knew all about the white man's world and knowledge, and who would now go to another land beyond, was not such a frequent occurrence that it could be taken lightly. Who knew but he might be interested in their daughter? Stranger things had happened. After all, learning was not the only thing. Though Wamuhu had no learning, yet charms she had and she could be trusted to captivate any young man's heart with her looks and smiles.

"You will sit down. Take that stool."

"No!" He noticed with bitterness that he did not call her "mother."

"Where is Wamuhu?" The mother threw a triumphant glance at her husband. They exchanged a knowing look. John bit his lips again and felt like bolting. He controlled himself with difficulty.

"She has gone out to get some tea leaves. Please sit down. She will cook you some tea when she comes."

"I am afraid . . ." he muttered some inaudible words and went out. He almost collided with Wamuhu.

In the hut:

"Didn't I tell you? Trust a woman's eye!"

"You don't know these young men."

"But you see John is different. Everyone speaks well of him and he is a clergyman's son."

"Y-e-e-s! A clergyman's son? You forget your daughter is circumcised." The old man was remembering his own day. He had found for himself a good, virtuous woman, initiated in all the tribe's ways. And she had known no other man. He had married her. They were happy. Other men of his *Rika* had done the same. All their girls had been virgins, it being a taboo to touch a girl in that way, even if you slept in the same bed, as indeed so many young men and girls did. Then the white men had come, preaching a strange religion, strange ways, which all men followed. The tribe's code of behavior was broken. The new faith could not keep the tribe together. How could it? The men who followed the new faith would not let the girls be circumcised. And they would not let their sons marry circumcised girls. Puu! Look at what was happening. Their young men went away to the land of the white men. What did they bring? White women. Black women who spoke English. Aaa— bad. And the young men who were left just did not mind. They made unmarried girls their wives and then left them with fatherless children.

"What does it matter?" his wife was replying. "Is Wamuhu not as good as the best of them? Anyway, John is different."

"Different! different! Puu! They are all alike. Those

coated with the white clay of the white man's ways are the worst. They have nothing inside. Nothing—nothing here." He took a piece of wood and nervously poked the dying fire. A strange numbness came over him. He trembled. And he feared; he feared for the tribe. For now he said it was not only the educated men who were coated with strange ways, but the whole tribe. The tribe had followed a false *Irimu* like the girl in the story. For the old man trembled and cried inside, mourning for a tribe that had crumbled. The tribe had nowhere to go to. And it could not be what it was before. He stopped poking and looked hard at the ground.

"I wonder why he came. I wonder." Then he looked at his wife and said, "Have you seen strange behavior with your daughter?"

His wife did not answer. She was preoccupied with her own great hopes . . .

John and Wamuhu walked on in silence. The intricate streets and turns were well known to them both. Wamuhu walked with quick light steps; John knew she was in a happy mood. His steps were heavy and he avoided people even though it was dark. But why should he feel ashamed? The girl was beautiful, probably the most beautiful girl in the whole of Limuru. Yet he feared being seen with her. It was all wrong. He knew that he could have loved her, even then he wondered if he did not love her. Perhaps it was hard to tell but had he been one of the young men he had met, he would not have hesitated in his answer.

Outside the village he stopped. She too stopped. Neither had spoken a word all through. Perhaps the silence spoke louder than words. Each was only too conscious of the other.

"Do they know?" Silence. Wamuhu was probably considering the question. "Don't keep me waiting. Please answer me," he implored. He felt weary, very weary, like an old man who had suddenly reached his journey's end.

"No. You told me to give you one more week. A week is over today."

"Yes. That's why I came!" John hoarsely whispered.

Wamuhu did not speak. John looked at her. Darkness was now between them. He was not really seeing her; before him was the image of his father—haughtily religious and dominating. Again he thought: I John, a priest's son, respected by all and going to college, will fall, fall to the ground. He did not want to contemplate the fall.

"It was your fault." He found himself accusing her. In his heart he knew he was lying.

"Why do you keep on telling me that? Don't you want to marry me?"

John sighed. He did not know what to do.

Once upon a time there was a young girl . . . she had no home to go to . . . she could not go forward to the beautiful land and see all the good things because the Irimu was on the way . . .

"When will you tell them?"

"Tonight." He felt desperate. Next week he would go to the college. If he could persuade her to wait, he might be able to get away and come back when the storm and consternation had abated. But then the government might withdraw his bursary. He was frightened and there was a sad note of appeal as he turned to her and said:

"Look, Wamuhu, how long have you been pre— I mean like this?"

"I have told you over and over again. I have been pregnant for three months and mother is being suspicious. Only yesterday she said I breathed like a woman with a child."

"Do you think you could wait for three weeks more?" She laughed. Ah! the little witch! She knew his trick. Her laughter always aroused many emotions in him.

"All right. Give me just tomorrow. I'll think up something. Tomorrow I'll let you know all."

"I agree. Tomorrow. I cannot wait any more unless you mean to marry me."

Why not marry her? She is beautiful! Why not marry her? And do I or don't I love her?

She left. John felt as if she was deliberately blackmailing him. His knees were weak and lost strength. He could not move but sank on the ground in a heap. Sweat poured profusely down his cheeks, as if he had been running hard under a strong sun. But this was cold sweat. He lay on the grass; he did not want to think. Oh! No! He could not possibly face his father. Or his mother. Or Rev. Thomas Carstone who had had such faith in him. John realized that he was not more secure than anybody else, in spite of his education. He was no better than Wamuhu. *Then why don't you marry her?* He did not know. John had grown up under a Calvinistic father and learnt under a Calvinistic headmaster—a missionary! John tried to pray. But to whom was he praying? To Carstone's God? It sounded false. It was as if he was blaspheming. Could he pray to the God of the tribe? His sense of guilt crushed him.

He woke up. Where was he? Then he understood. Wamuhu had left him. She had given him one day. He stood up; he felt good. Weakly, he began to walk back home. It was lucky that darkness blanketed the whole earth, and him in it. From the various huts, he could hear laughter, heated talks or quarrels. Little fires could be seen flickeringly red through the open doors. Village stars —John thought. He raised up his eyes. The heavenly stars, cold and distant, looked down on him, impersonally. Here and there, groups of boys and girls could be heard laughing and shouting. For them life seemed to go on as usual. John consoled himself by thinking that they too would come to face their day of trial.

John was shaky. Why! Why! Why could he not defy all expectations, all prospects of a future, and marry the girl? No. No. It was impossible. She was circumcised, and he knew that his father and the church would never consent to such a marriage. She had no learning, or rather she had not gone beyond Standard 4. Marrying her would probably ruin his chances of ever going to a University. . . .

He tried to move briskly. His strength had returned. His imagination and thought took flight. He was trying to explain his action before an accusing world—he had done so many times before, ever since he knew of this. He still wondered what he could have done. The girl had attracted him. She was graceful and her smile had been very bewitching. There was none who could equal her and no girl in the village had any pretence to any higher standard of education. Women's education was very low. Perhaps that was why so many Africans went "away" and came back married. He too wished he had gone with the others, especially in the last giant student airlift to America. If only Wamuhu had learning . . . and she was uncircumcised . . . then he might probably rebel. . . .

The light still shone in his mother's hut. John wondered if he should go in for the night prayers. But he thought against it; he might not be strong enough to face his parents. In his hut, the light had gone out. He hoped his father had not noticed it . . .

John woke up early. He was frightened. He was normally not superstitious but still he did not like the dreams of the night. He dreamt of circumcision; he had just been initiated in the tribal manner. Somebody—he could not tell his face—came and led him because he took pity on him. They went, went into a strange land. Somehow, he found himself alone. The somebody had vanished. A ghost came. He recognized it as the ghost of the home he had left. It pulled him back; then another ghost came. It was the ghost of the land he had come to. It pulled him from the front. The two contested. Then came other ghosts from all sides and pulled him from all sides so that his body began to fall into pieces. And the ghosts were unsubstantial. He could not cling to any. Only they were pulling him, and he was becoming nothing, nothing . . . he was now standing a distance away. It had not been him. But he was looking at the girl, the girl in the story. She had nowhere to go. He thought he would go to help her; he would show her the way. But as he went to her, he lost his way . . . he was all alone . . . something destructive was coming towards him, coming, coming . . . He woke up. He was sweating all over—

Dreams about circumcision were no good. They portended death. He dismissed the dream with a laugh. He opened the window only to find the whole country clouded in mist. It was perfect July weather in Limuru. The hills, ridges, valleys and plains that surrounded the village were lost in the mist. It looked such a strange place. But there was almost a magic fascination in it. Limuru was a land of contrasts and evoked differing emotions, at different times. Once, John would be fascinated, and would yearn to touch the land, embrace it or just be on the grass. At another time he would feel repelled by the dust, the strong sun and the pot-holed roads. If only his struggle were just against the dust, the mist, the sun and the rain, he might feel content. Content to live here. At least he thought he would never like to die and be buried anywhere else but at Limuru. But there was the human element whose vices and betrayal of other men were embodied as the new ugly villages. The last night's incident rushed into his mind like a flood, making him weak again. He came out of his blankets and went out. Today he would go to the shops. He was uneasy. An odd feeling was coming to him, in fact had been coming, that his relationship with his father was perhaps unnatural. But he dismissed the thought. Tonight would be the "day of reckoning." He shuddered to think of it. It was unfortunate that this scar had come into his life at this time when he was going to Makerere and it would have brought him closer to his father.

They went to the shops. All day long, John remained quiet as they moved from shop to shop buying things from the lanky but wistful Indian traders. And all day long, John wondered why he feared his father so much. He had grown up fearing him, trembling whenever he spoke or gave commands. John was not alone in this.

Stanley was feared by all.

He preached with great vigor, defying the very gates of hell. Even during the Emergency, he had gone on preaching, scolding, judging and condemning. All those who were not saved were destined for hell. Above all, Stanley was known for his great moral observances—a bit too strict, rather pharisaical in nature. None noticed this; certainly not the sheep he shepherded. If an elder broke any of the rules, he was liable to be expelled, or excommunicated. Young men and women, seen standing together "in a manner prejudicial to church and God's morality" (they were one anyway), were liable to be excommunicated. And so, many young men tried to serve two masters, by seeing their girls at night and going to church by day. The alternative was to give up church-going altogether . . .

Stanley took a fatherly attitude to all the people in the village. You must be strict with what is yours. And because of all this, he wanted his house to be a good example. That is why he wanted his son to grow up right. But motives behind many human actions may be mixed. He could never forget that he had also fallen before his marriage. Stanley was also a product of the disintegration of the tribe due to the new influences.

The shopping took a long time. His father strictly observed the silences between them and neither by word nor by hint did he refer to last night. They reached home and John was thinking that all was well when his father called him.

"John."

"Yes, father."

"Why did you not come for prayers last night?"

"I forgot—"

"Where were you?"

Why do you ask me? What right have you to know where I was? One day I am going to revolt against you. But immediately, John knew that this act of rebellion was something beyond him—not unless something happened to push him into it. It needed someone with something he lacked.

"I-I-I mean, I was—"

"You should not sleep so early before prayers. Remember to be there tonight."

"I will."

Something in the boy's voice made the father look up. John went away relieved. All was still well.

Evening came. John dressed like the night before and walked with faltering steps towards the fatal place. The night of reckoning had come. And he had not thought of anything. After this night all would know. Even Rev. Thomas Carstone would hear of it. He remembered Mr. Carstone and the last words of blessing he had spoken to him. No! he did not want to remember. It was no good remembering these things; and yet the words came. They were clearly written in the air, or in the darkness of his mind. "You are going into the world. The world is waiting even like a hungry lion, to swallow you, to devour you. Therefore, beware of the world. Jesus said, Hold fast unto. . . ." John felt a pain—a pain that wriggled through his flesh as he remembered these words. He contemplated the coming fall. Yes! He, John would fall from the Gates of Heaven down through the open waiting gates of Hell. Ah! He could see it all, and what people would say. Everybody would shun his company, would give him oblique looks that told so much. The trouble with John was that his imagination magnified the fall from the heights of "goodness" out of proportion. And fear of people and consequences ranked high in the things that made him contemplate the fall with so much horror.

John devised all sorts of punishment for himself. And when it came to thinking of a way out, only fantastic and impossible ways of escape came into his head. He simply could not make up his mind. And because he could not and he feared father and people, and he did not know his true attitude to the girl, he came to the agreed spot having nothing to tell the girl. Whatever he did looked fatal to him. Then suddenly he said—

"Look Wamuhu. Let me give you money. You might then say that someone else was responsible. Lots of girls have done this. Then that man may marry you. For me, it is impossible. You know that."

"No. I cannot do that. How can you, you—"

"I will give you two hundred shillings."

"No!"

"Three hundred!"

"No!" She was almost crying. It pained her to see him so.

"Four hundred, five hundred, six hundred!" John had begun calmly but now his voice was running high. He was excited. He was becoming more desperate. Did he know what he was talking about? He spoke quickly, breathlessly, as if he was in a hurry. The figure was rapidly rising—nine thousand, ten thousand, twenty thousand . . . He is mad. He is foaming. He is quickly moving towards the girl in the dark. He has laid his hands on her shoulders and is madly imploring her in a hoarse voice. Deep inside him, something horrid that assumes the threatening anger of his father and the village, seems to be pushing him. He is violently shaking Wamuhu, while his mind tells him that he is patting her gently. Yes. He is out of his mind. The figure has now reached fifty thousand shillings and is increasing. Wamuhu is afraid, extricates herself from him, the mad, educated son of a religious clergyman, and she runs. He runs after her and holds her, calling her by all sorts of endearing words. But he is shaking her, shake, shake, her, her—he tries to hug her by the neck, presses

. . . She lets out one horrible scream and then falls on the ground. And so all of a sudden, the struggle is over, the figures stop and John stands there trembling like the leaf of a tree on a windy day.

John, in the grip of fear, ran homeward. Soon everyone would know.

Mulyankota

Nuwa Sentongo

Nuwa Sentongo was born in Uganda in 1942.
He received his B.A. in 1968 from Makerere University College, where he was active in the theater.
His short stories and poems have been published in
several East African publications. In September of
1968, Mr. Sentongo began graduate work at Indiana University in the Folklore Institute.

His name had spread far and wide as the greatest
eater the world had ever known. He could eat a meal
intended for ten people just by himself. Yet he did not
grow a belly. His belly was not at all noticeable, nor
were his buttocks. It seemed that his stomach was like a
huge fire; however much wood you may add to it, it consumes it all and does not get satisfied. All his neighbors
feared him. They thought that he probably was diseased
because a human being could not eat like he did. These
neighbors would not have anything to do with him; not
even as little as talk to him. But, poor man, he needed
friendship. He wished that his neighbors could talk to him
directly rather than backbite him. He even imagined that
someone spitting in his face would be reacting in a much
better way than those statue-like neighbors who tried
as much as possible to have nothing to do with him.

One day when he was fed up with his neighbors' indifference, he decided to provoke Mr. Afu by staying next to his house. He had not intended to stay there long, at least he told Mr. and Mrs. Afu, but while he was there in their house it began to pour cats and dogs. As a result, Mulyankota (for that was his name) was forced to stay till meal time. Mrs. Afu was such a resourceful housewife that she devised ways and means of curing Mulyankota's unnatural hunger. First she tried to give him some coffee. She brought it in a fifteen cup coffee-pot, and waited on him, pouring cup after cup. She grew tired of pouring out coffee at Mulyankota's unnatural speed, and she made it clear to him that henceforth it was to be a self-service system. Mulyankota was not in the least affected. As a matter of fact he was overjoyed because then he could regulate his speed in the way he wanted. Therefore it was not accidental that shortly after Mrs. Afu had surrendered the pot to him, he drained it and declared jovially, "I thank you very much Mrs. Afu for your wonderful coffee. It has been really delicious. I haven't drank coffee for such a long time. I think I last drank coffee when my first wife was cooking for me. In any case her coffee wasn't as good as yours, and unfortunately with me coffee is the proverb with which words are eaten. I can't talk without coffee. I wish I could drink some more. It has really been good coffee."

"Did you like it?" asked Mrs. Afu. "If you like I will bring you some more."

"By all means," Mulyankota answered, handing over both the cup and the pot. But Mrs. Afu only took the pot. She did not feel like taking the cup.

The period between the arrival of the second lot of coffee passed without any remarkable happenings. Afu and Mulyankota made a few remarks about the rain, but said nothing really serious. And, surprisingly, Mrs. Afu came back almost as soon as she left. It seemed as if she had prepared herself for Mulyankota's second lot of coffee. She brought another fifteen cups and this time handed the pot over to Mulyankota to help himself. It was such an awkward moment, because Mulyankota concentrated on his coffee and forgot the presence of his hosts. His hosts made faces at each other, winked at each other, but otherwise they remained silent. To their amazement, he drained the coffee pot, and made a somewhat comic remark: "I don't know what has happened to me today. When I drink, all the coffee just disappears and I don't know where it goes. My stomach is as empty as it was when I started to drink this coffee."

But Mrs. Afu was already disgusted with his insatiable, unnatural hunger. As it was already meal time she had calculated that if she offered him coffee before the meal, he probably would eat something near a normal amount of food. But lo! She had misfired. Yet her husband was grunting with hunger. She must bring food. Mulyankota or no Mulyankota. The rain outside had not subsided at all, so Mulyankota could not terminate his visit. Thus Mrs. Afu was forced to bring the food in spite of everything. However, she tried her last trick. There were remains-over of the previous meal and these were almost twice as much as the freshly cooked meal. She decided to offer the remains-over to Mulyankota while she and her husband enjoyed the freshly cooked food. She did not even warm it; it was cold and hard and unfresh because they had no fridge in which to keep it.

Yet Mulyankota enjoyed every morsel of it. He gobbled it and finished before his hosts had gone halfway through their meal. As a matter of fact, he said that it was the best food he had ever tasted; that all those women he had been marrying did not know how to cook good food. Mrs. Afu was not embarrassed by Mulyankota's remarks because she had become familiar with his peculiarity. On the other hand, Mr. Afu understood the meaninglessness of Mulyankota's gratitude; but he, at the same time, wondered why a man should decide to behave as Mulyankota behaved. However, Mulyankota's superfluous gratitude earned him a reward. Mrs. Afu gave him a considerable amount of food from the fresh meal. No sooner had he tasted this food than he announced jovially that a little dose from that dish was enough to send him to heaven; that he had never thought of heaven until he tasted that food; that when he tasted that food he imagined that heaven must be the only place where people eat such delicious food. In short he imagined himself to be in heaven. His remarks had no impact on his hosts because they were already fed up with his words. The rest of the meal was eaten in silence. Therefore, it is not surprising that he left immediately after the meal, although it was still raining.

Mrs. Afu began to curse herself for having entertained him. She realized that she had fallen victim to his calculations. He came in at the right time just to have a meal, and, of course, he was assisted by the skies which sent down heavy rain. However, she vowed never to forgive him for eating so much and never to forgive herself having entertained him. As for Mr. Afu, he just wished he could strangle Mulyankota there and then while he was gobbling the food. But after a while, the thought left him and he began to think of Mulyankota as an unfortunate human being who needed a wife to look after him. Indeed Mulyankota was unfortunate and deserved pity.

There were times when he used to get women. They would come, but would go as soon as they came. No woman would stand his habits, especially his large insatiable appetite. Whenever opportunity offered itself, he would buy some meat, but he would buy two separate parcels: one for himself and the other for his wife if there was any at home, and his was always three times as big. He would eat all his meat at one meal while his wife preserved some for the next meal. Then at the following meal he would demand that meat which his wife had kept for herself. If the wife refused to surrender the meat, she would be beaten till she submitted to her husband's will. In fact he would give her a summon on the husband's will. He might even force her to admit that the moon is green. On the other hand, although Mulyankota really ate a lot, he probably was, at the same time, the laziest man in the village. At night he would eat so much that, like a python, he would sleep like a log. His wife, if there was any around, would wake up early to go and toil in the garden. Then around eleven o'clock, he would wake up and look for his wife wherever she might be in the garden and demand food. He would order her to stop whatever she would be doing and order her to give him food immediately. But then after eating an incredible amount of food, he would start quarrelling that the wife was lazy, that she had cultivated only a tiny area, and that soon they would run out of food. And they often did.

His first wife was very understanding. He had been told that she was a very hard-working woman and so would grow enough food for him. Indeed she was a very hard-working woman and she was still a maid. He married her quietly. Greedy as he was, he avoided feasts of any sort, lest he would let the tiger loose. This woman, Natalia, used to toil hard in the garden, mornings and afternoons, bearing her husband's rebukes that she was lazy both in the garden and in her feminine obligations. He overworked her in both areas. Everyday she worked even harder, telling herself, "Toil like a slave and eat like a lady," but that glorious saying never came true. After one year of toiling outdoors and indoors, day and night, she was so worn out that she decided to complain to her parents. If her parents had been hard-hearted, they obviously would have been moved by her wizened appearance. She did not even try to plead with them. They were hypersympathetic and called Mulyankota immediately.

As a test, they prepared a huge meal for him. They

slaughtered two huge roosters and prepared a huge meal of matoke for him. To their amazement, he ate and finished whatever they offered him. Natalia pointed out to her parents: "You see, that's how he always eats. I work alone in the garden while he is in bed snoring. When he wakes up, he begins to harass me and I have to feed him with such amounts of food. And at night he never allows me any sleep. When he begins, he goes on and on like the way he eats. I can't bear it any more."

His parents-in-law told him that he was not a human being but a monster and therefore unfit for their daughter. And that since he had not paid them any brideprice, he had no demands to make but to leave them and their daughter in peace. That he did. He left, despondently, worried how he would manage his stomach without a wife. Fortunately for Natalia, they had had no marital fruits so she would have no blood ties to him. A clouded future lay ahead of him.

After Natalia he tried hard with various women. He would get a woman and she would stay only for one month, then disappear. The villagers watched him pine away as they made unsympathetic comments. Any new wife he might get would hear all sorts of stories about him from other village women. Some of these wives would ask him whether the stories they had heard were true. Over a period of about five years after the departure of his first wife, he brought twenty different wives. But none of them would stay for a respectable length of time. However, he never gave up. He kept on trying different women, hoping that perhaps out of those one might stay. So he hunted all the time. He went to remote villages, where, he hoped, stories about him might not have reached.

One day, about one year after his memorable visit to the Afus, he set out early in the morning determined to get himself a wife. He vowed not to return without a wife and that the wife must be a very obedient one. He had no particular destination in mind. He just took a path which happened to be nearest to his house. He followed it almost aimlessly in spite of his vow. As he trotted down the path, a chameleon warned him, "Haste is all right, but caution is also a good thing." However, his attention was drawn to a toad which made a more favorable confession: "Waiting for tomorrow caused me to remain without a tail." Mulyankota remembered the motto which regulated his life all the time: "He who is quick, catches the white ants." With that motto he fixed his eyes on the path and paid no attention to the chameleon's nonsense.

He went into a far distant land, and reached a point at which he could not decide whether to go ahead or to return. Fortunately enough, his indecision was rewarded when a charming young girl came strolling down the path. He reassured himself, "A young girl is like a bushbuck, every hunter tries his luck." He immediately waylaid her, and after tremendous courting she agreed to go with him to his home. But first she had to fetch a parcel of her immediate requirements and she preferred to go unaccompanied. He wished he had some powers to cause the parcel to be brought without her having to go away. He consoled himself, "A patient mouse in a new plot may one day eat a ripe banana." However, he did not have to console himself for a long time because the young girl came back almost as soon as she left. She carried on her head a huge parcel which she claimed was food. Naturally Mulyankota was more than happy when he learned that it was food she was carrying. The journey back home was shorter and more comfortable because he had somebody to talk to.

On the way he discovered that her name was Nvannungi, but beyond that she was not willing to discuss her private life. Neither did he want to because he feared that such a discussion might lead her to probe into his private life and discover that he was a gourmand. Thus their conversation on the way was very general and evasive; as a matter of fact one might say that it was not worth noting. When they arrived home, Nvannungi prepared a small amount of food for their dinner. Her husband started to rebuke her, that she was inconsiderate. After such a long journey, he needed a big mountain of food. But she turned a deaf ear to all his rebukes. And he feared to offend her on the first day because he had suffered enough those several months he had spent without a woman. He calculated that when she brought the food, he would just grab it all to himself and leave her nothing. When the food was brought, he felt all his strength oozing out of his body. He could not even grab his wife's share as he had planned. And the small amount he got was barely enough to fill up his stomach.

When they retired to bed, they played the game for a short time, and surprisingly he got so exhausted that he just collapsed. But his wife was wide awake. She rose up from the bed and went outside, naked. She started dancing round the house, many times, then in the garden and in the neighbours' gardens. She came back to the house and called in a callous voice, "Mulyankota, Mulyankota!" In his half-deafness, Mulyankota answered feebly to the call of her voice, but his body was too weak to move. Nvannungi observed, "Yes, he is willing and is easy to master. Only one more thing and he will be subdued." When she came back into the house she tied a package of sorghum into the roof, put on her nightgown and finally joined her husband in bed. He did not in the least know or even suspect that she had left him in bed and gone outside naked. She woke up early the following morning and went to work in the garden. She worked hard and covered a large area.

She came back and prepared lunch. Mulyankota was still in bed. When lunch was ready, she persuaded him to wake up, which he did very unwillingly. She spoke to him very sweetly while he washed his face. Then suddenly he demanded food. He must eat. He had to eat. She brought the food obligingly. The food was such a small amount that he wanted to slap her for her impudence in trying to starve him. She jumped, screamed, and pointed up in the roof. He looked up in the roof, at the package of sorghum, and became powerless. He could not say a word. He simply collapsed in the chair and waited for the food. Nvannungi offered him the food. He ate only a tiny amount and said his stomach was full. He looked around the room, and it seemed to be full of ghosts. He turned to his wife; she was very delicious and appetizing. He whisked her off to bed and they had a good time. This time he got his satisfaction, something he had never got in all his life. It was satisfaction without exhaustion. He had not overworked himself or his partner. He enjoyed the experience at first. But after sometime, he felt uneasy. He felt that his aggressive appetite, his aggressive greed, his aggressive laziness, his aggressive command of himself, and all his other aggressives were gradually leaving him.

Every hour, every minute, every tiny second seemed to be stealing away his aggressiveness. He sauntered through his courtyard like a wet chicken seeking shelter from a rainstorm. Whenever he looked at Nvannungi, he saw that miraculous beauty radiating, but its radiance had something ominous about it. It was some sort of sweet force which seduces you to lose a battle, some sort of Homeric siren. She was not domineering, at least she did not seem to be domineering for the present. Yet she seemed to be taking away his aggressiveness by some invisible power. And he was willing because it was all right to be powerless provided he was in sweet hands. Anyhow he seemed to enjoy Nvannungi's presence which had already become indispensable.

At night he felt so strange that he hardly tasted his food. He felt better afterwards, though. Then they went to bed. As on the previous night, his wife was wide awake. She left the bed, naked, went out, started dancing round the house many times, then in the garden and in the neighbors' gardens. She came back, just outside the house and called out, "Mulyankota, Mulyankota!" He heard the call very clearly. Not only did he answer but he walked out of bed and followed his wife outside, naked. He joined his wife without knowing what he was doing. He was not himself any more. He was possessed by the night-dancing cult. They both danced together round the house many times, then in their garden and in their neighbors' gardens. They went further and further, beyond the village, and yet far beyond.

Something seemed to be drawing them towards it, something so powerful that they both could not resist. It did not feel dangerous or cumbersome, nor did they offer any resistance, nor did they want to offer any resistance. As a matter of fact it was a pleasure to be pulled by this mighty, sweet force. Further and further, from village to village over the hills, through the valleys, over rivers, through thick forests, they went by leaps and bounds. They did not feel exhausted. They regenerated some strange energy which kept them going faster and even faster. After running for a long time, they seemed to be drawing to the source of the force that was pulling them. It felt even mightier as they leaped wildly and madly. Suddenly they came to a halt. There they were, right on the edge of a grave, with a corpse staring at them. It was ready, waiting for them to take it. It must have been the smell of that dead human flesh that was drawing them to the place.

But lo! Another party of night-dancers had already been there before Mulyankota and Nvannungi. The other night-dancers were responsible for calling the corpse from its grave. It was a party of four strong men, flames of fire issuing from their mouths, carrying human bones as their weapons. Both parties faced each other and it appeared that a big fight might break out, and it would be the doom of the night-dancers. The party which had human bones hit the bones together. As the bones clattered, they issued flames of fire. With these fires lighting the way, the four night-dancers closed in upon Mulyankota and Nvannungi. Unfortunately, they had carried no weapons.

Nvannungi became really frantic as she applied her magic. She wriggled through one of the men's legs and disappeared into the darkness of the night. Mulyankota was helpless. It was Nvannungi's cult which had possessed him and caused him to be pulled by the dead human flesh. When Nvannungi wriggled away, the cult also wriggled away. He became exhausted. The four night-dancers attacked, but he did not retaliate. Realizing his submission, the night-dancers did not inflict much physical pain onto him. Instead, they ordered him to carry the corpse. Now that the cult had left him, he could not bear the smell of dead, rotten human flesh. He wanted to be sick, but he could not be sick. His stomach became very tight as if it were full of gas. The corpse was slimy and so rotten that some of its parts were falling off. But the night-dancers picked them up and stored them carefully. Mulyankota had never been through anything like it all his life. The corpse was literally uncarriable.

Although it was a cold night, Mulyankota was sweating under the heavy burden and panting for fresh air. It was during this journey, bearing this burden of a corpse, that he coordinated his senses and came to the realization that Nvannungi was a night-dancer. The logical conclusion he arrived at was that she had betrayed him to the night-dancers to eat him. The possibilities of their being her relatives and this being her village could not be ruled out completely since Mulyankota could not tell in what part of the world he happened to be at that particular moment.

Then began a moment of serious thinking. What could he do in order to escape? He could not escape by running away because night-dancers run faster than the wind. Besides, he was very exhausted. Even if he were to run away, he did not know where to go because he did not know that part of the country. So he trusted to luck. There was not much to see or tell about the journey because it was pitch dark. Now and then he wanted to throw down the corpse, as his chest and his muscles threatened to burst under the heavy weight. But he held out for about an hour; then they arrived at a village in that dead of the night.

He was led into a house and ordered to lay the corpse down. Still in the dark, he was warned to be prepared to shave the corpse's hair. He did not argue but pointed out that it would be much more convenient if he fetched some banana leaves onto which he would throw the hair. The night-dancers gave him permission to go and fetch the banana leaves from outside. While laying down the corpse, he had knelt down on his left leg and had felt something like a mat. He grabbed what he thought was the mat and went out with it pretending to fetch the banana leaves.

As soon as he estimated to be out of their hearing, he began to run as fast as his legs could carry him. It was after he had covered some distance that he took a rest. Then he felt the thing he carried with him and discovered it was a piece of barkcloth. He tied it round his waist. He hated resting because he could never tell what such a night would bring him. So he resumed his journey, going nowhere, for he did not know where he was going, nor could he tell where he was. He could not tell whether he was in a forest or a bush or a coffee garden because it was pitch dark. He kept on going in the direction he thought was ahead of him. But he might have been going backwards to where he was running from, directly into the night-dancers' arms; or he might have been heading into a lion's den.

He must have gone on like that for about an hour when suddenly he found himself in the middle of a big assembly of people. He knew they were people, because he heard them talk, and he understood what they were saying. They were saying that there must be a stranger among them who had caused all the trouble. Therefore they must search, find, and arrest the stranger and take him to the chief; then things would go back to normal. The man whom Mulyankota thought must be the chief consented in a deep voice. He ordered his army of dogs to be let out and smell the stranger.

It did not take the dogs a long time to smell Mulyankota. When they came to him, they started to bark frantically at him and he felt strong arms grabbing him from all sides and dragging him along. The dogs led the way barking in a chorus. The dogs led their victim to the chief where Mulyankota had to face serious charges. Had he known that he was going to be tried for a crime he had never committed, he probably would not have been as scared as he was. But all the time he had a justifiable suspicion that probably after the dogs it would be leopards, and lions and god knows what! Thus he held his heart in his teeth ready to chew it in case of extreme necessity, and if possible pass away. Soon they were in front of the chief because he sensed that they must have reached some person of authority. The dogs began to growl, expecting to be thanked. The chief thanked them. One of the people holding Mulyankota announced to the chief, "Your highness, the chief's drums don't sound for nothing; the chief's dogs don't bark for nothing; the chief's banana leaves don't shake for nothing. When the fire goes out, then we know something is wrong; we know there will be famine, because the fire fertilizes our land. Your highness, when the chief's hunters go on a hunt, they always catch something; we have caught the offender and here he is."

With his hands, the chief felt Mulyankota's body from head to toe, then began to interrogate him: "Do you admit that you have committed the crime?"

"Which crime, sir?" asked Mulyankota.

The villagers grumbled that Mulyankota was belittling

their chief. How could he answer the chief like that? The chief silenced them and continued, "Perhaps you don't know yet. Perhaps you know already, and that's why you committed the crime. However, it doesn't make any difference to me; I will tell you the story from the beginning. We people of Bwaya use fire not only to give us light and to cook food, but also to fertilize our soil and to protect us from the lust of the night-dancers of Bidibo. Those night-dancers don't like our fire because it protects our flesh from them. Two days ago one of them must have played a trick on us and stole away our fire. And yesterday my assistant was killed and I understand those night-dancers have eaten him. Since you are a stranger, you must belong to the side of the night-dancers and we want you to give us back our fire. When I felt your body, I realized that you are wearing something, and you are not naked as the other night-dancers. But, whether you are a night-dancer or not, we know you must be coming from Bidibo village because of the smell of your barkcloth. Therefore we ask you to give us back our fire so that we may fertilize our soil."

"But," protested Mulyankota, "fire doesn't fertilize the land. . . ." His words were swallowed up by the shouts from the villagers, shouts of "Blasphemy," "sacrilege," "burn him," "hang him . . ."

The chief silenced them: "Quiet, my friends; quiet, my people. I know this man before us has committed the worst crime anybody can commit. It is more than treason and is punishable with death. It is a sacrilege to say that fire doesn't fertilize our land. Furthermore, the fact that you said that the fire doesn't fertilize our land confirms your guilt that you are responsible for the disappearance of our fire. You wanted to test if our land will remain fertile without the fire. I would like to draw your attention to another law here that any kind of theft carries capital punishment. So your sentence cannot be less than death. But my dear villagers, I appeal to your reason.

We want to punish this man with a really painful death, something like burning him or hanging him by the rope or let him be eaten by a wild animal. My dogs are so trained that they cannot tear human flesh to death. We have no fire to burn him with and we have no light to enable us to hang him by the rope. Even if we were to kill him off like that, which we can do by beating him, we won't have solved our problem, because we will still need the fire. Therefore, the most important thing is for us to force him to give us back our fire."

At that point, a group of people who had been guarding the border of Bwaya arrived and felt their way through the crowd to the chief. In their search for the chief they were guided by the chief's voice. They pushed their way through the crowd and reached the chief. Their leader announced their presence and mission: "Your highness, I am Kacweke, the son of Tebyasa, grandson of Byakonye, great-grandson of Bikajjo, great-great-grandson of Mpum-umpu. I belong to the mantis clan, and the monkey's liver is my totem. Our clan-head Mudumu is a great man and he looks after your drums. My grandfather, Byakonye, was a loyal servant to your father, chief Dudubu. When he died, my father, Tebyasa, served your father, chief Dudubu. When your father died, my father served you for a long time until his death, and then you appointed me in his stead. I have been your loyal servant for now two weeks watching over the border. I have been watching over our border with Bugwayo, son of Dankwina, grandson of Gondolo. Bugwayo is a member of the centipede clan and their totem is the snail horns. The centipede clan-head is responsible for brewing your banana-beer. Another guard with me is Jojo son of Gwala, grandson of Maddu. He belongs to the cockroach clan and is your great blacksmith. We were watching over the border when all the fire suddenly went out and everything became dark. It was so pitch dark that we couldn't see each other. So we kept together by holding onto each others' arms. But after a long while, which might have been a day or two (heaven knows how long it was; it seemed like million years), we spied a small fire, smoldering in the direction of the Bundiguru hills. We decided to follow the fire. We followed it for a long time. I can't tell for how long; I had never known that without fire one loses one's sense of time; anyway, after a long time, we saw the fire settle in one place. We waited to see what would happen. The little fire kindled other fires and soon the whole place was lighted up. To our amazement, we saw a rhinoceros standing in the middle of a cave with the smoldering fire on its horn. It sneezed and sighed and laughed extravagantly, and then boasted, 'Well, let them suffer. They don't like me, those human beings. They say I am ugly. They want to cut down the bush and plant their crops here in my home, right here. They want to destroy my home. O.K., now I have taken their fire, what can they do? I will not give this fire away.'

"Your highness, we conferred among ourselves, wondering what to do. The general opinion was that we come back and get the necessary reinforcements to attack the rhino. But of course we could not figure out our way in that darkness. While we were arguing which way was likely to be the right one, the rhino smelt us and called out, 'Ho, ho, ho you human beings, come here before I attack you. I have smelled you already and if you think you can escape in that pitch dark, try it and see. But I warn you, if you do, then know that you will lose your lives.'

"Your highness, we had no alternative but to obey the rhino. We went to its den. It scrutinized us and asked us what we were doing in its kingdom. We told it that we had spied its fire and wanted to take some of it back to the village. At that, the rhino asked us to tell it a story which would make it laugh, but none of us had any story to tell. So it dismissed us, but not without a warning that in future whoever dares to face it without a story to make it laugh will be killed. Your highness that's the news we bring to the people of Bwaya. In one way it's bad news, but in another, good news because now we know who stole our fire and we know where it is. Perhaps among your people there are some who can tell an interesting story that will make the rhino laugh."

It is true there were many people in Bwaya who could tell stories and make even the saddest person laugh. There was Bugigi who, they said, when he told stories would cause mice to lose their way, assuming they were going somewhere. There was Zaduku who caused people to laugh at their mothers' funerals. But none of these people was willing to face the rhino, and since it was pitch dark, there was no chance of forcing them to volunteer once they decided to hide. Therefore, the chief turned to his captive Mulyankota and told him to go to the rhino to fetch the fire. If he got himself eaten by the rhino that would be his business. Mulyankota was led away by the three guards who by now knew the way to the rhino's den. They tried to involve him in conversation, but his mind was away, thinking what sort of story he could tell the rhino.

He had no stories except his personal adventures which he did not regard in any way exciting. He tried to recall his childhood fireside stories, but none of them was exciting enough to cause the rhino to laugh. Failing everything, he came to the conclusion that he was walking into a death trap and might as well give up any hope for life. When they came to the point from where they saw the rhino's light, the leader of the group said, "Well, Mulyankota, we can't escort you any farther than this. That light you see there is in the rhino's den. So you just follow the light and you will meet the rhino. You will have to go the rest of the journey by yourself. Although the chief did not order us to wait for you, we feel that we should wait for you here. You will find us right here."

Mulyankota moved towards the light; he was blank as

if in a trance. No sooner had he left than the guards quickly ran back to the village, fearing the wrath of the rhino.

"Who's there?" the rhino asked in a cruel voice.

"A friend," Mulyankota answered in a cowardly voice.

"Which friend?" demanded the rhino.

"Well . . . ah . . . eh . . . h . . ."

While he was still floundering for words, the rhino sent a loud roar which almost caused Mulyankota to wet his pants, except that he was not wearing pants, he was wearing barkcloth. Then dead silence. He wondered what would happen next.

"Eh, human being, are you still there?" The rhino expected him to have run away.

"Yes," Mulyankota answered.

"O.K., come along." He went in nervously and sat down, at a distance from the rhino.

"What brings you here?" the rhino inquired.

"Well," Mulyankota stammered. "Well, I am a traveler. I have been traveling for now thirty years without any rest."

"Traveling thirty years without any rest! You tell lies, human being. I knew it. I should have known better. All human beings tell lies."

"No, sir, I am not lying to you," Mulyankota pleaded.

"O.K., if you have been traveling where are you going, tell me that?"

"Well, I don't know where I am going, and I don't know where I am coming from. But I have to travel because I have never reached my destination. I don't know this destination but I think I will know it when I reach it. So I have to keep on traveling. And now I am on one of my wanderings. When I saw this light, I thought I might come in and ask the owner of the fire to allow me to spend the night here. Maybe you will permit me to spend the night here, then I will continue with my journey tomorrow."

"Feel at home Mr. Traveler. What's your name?"

"My name is Mulyankota."

"Mulya . . . what?"

"Mu-lya-nko-ta." *

"Mulyankota! Ho, ho, that's really funny. Is it your real name?"

"It is not my real name. It is what the villagers call me, and I have accepted it, so I don't mind."

"Well, why do the villagers call you that?"

"I will tell you. I am a great gourmand. I can eat any amount of food without getting satisfied. Sometimes when I am slightly upset, I eat only a little amount, for instance an amount intended for fifteen people. Such an amount satisfies me only if I am upset and have a limitable appetite. One day when my in-laws offered me two huge roosters, I ate them and felt no change; I wished they had given me twenty of them. When one mean housewife offered me thirty cups of coffee and a damn meal of rotten stale food, I ate them all, although I thought there

---

* One who eats a whole bunch of bananas: Ganda (East Africa)—Ed.

were things which tasted like maggots in her stale food. I am like that. I just eat and eat . . ."

Before Mulyankota finished his explanation, the rhino was already rolling on the ground with laughter. It closed its eyes and laughed wildly. It roared. It rolled on the ground over and over, on its sides, its back, its posterior, then the horn. When the horn touched the ground, a cluster of burning material fell from it. Mulyankota carefully picked up the cluster of burning material and walked out stealthily. As soon as he thought he was out of hearing distance, he began to run as fast as his legs could carry him. He reached the village more dead than alive.

The villagers saw him arrive, holding a firebrand. The three guards wished they had waited for him on the way, ambushed him, and taken the firebrand away from him.

They wished they could claim the heroic deed for themselves. However, they had missed their chance. The chief received the brand and lighted his compound. For the first time in what seemed years, Mulyankota was able to use his eyes. But he could not see many things because his eyes were fixed on a charming young girl, apparently the chief's daughter.

She was standing next to the chief, rather absorbed in herself. She did not seem to care about, let alone understand what was going on. She had that introspective innocence which some people call absent-mindedness. Her large eyes stared as if in a dream, concentrating on one spot, yet not seeming to take notice of the spot. The spot might as well not have been there. Her eyes were not lifeless. They were full of vitality, but it was submissive vitality and it seemed to be riding somewhere in the skies. Yet Mulyankota noted this submissiveness, that although all the other people were chasing off mosquitoes from their bodies she allowed them to feast on hers. Probably she was not even aware of them. Mulyankota desired her submissiveness. He longed for it. He had to have it. The chief looked at her, but she took no notice of him. She seemed to be one of those characters in any fairy tale. Mulyankota was bothered. Is she real? Does she exist? Can she be provoked?

The chief spoke to Mulyankota: "On behalf of my people I thank you for having retrieved our fire. You will be gratified to hear that I exonerate you from the charge that you conspired with the Bidibo night-dancers to steal our fire since my guards have made it clear that it was the rhino who stole the fire. I see something in your face, something like a mark of honesty. Since you are an honest man I would like to invite you to stay with us here."

As if waking from a dream, Mulyankota slowly moved his eyes from the chief's daughter to the chief himself. He replied to the chief's compliment, "Your highness, with due respect for your hospitality, I am sincerely sorry that I have to turn down your warm-hearted invitation, because I have my property in the village where I come from, and I must go back to look after it."

Actually it was not the property which Mulyankota was thinking of, for he could get more property if he stayed and married the chief's daughter. But he feared that if he stayed he probably would soon fall out of favor on account of being a gourmand. The chief asked him if he could do anything to help him. When this question was asked, Mulyankota's eyes flashed onto the chief's daughter. He was not aware that he was now the center of attraction. Everybody was scrutinizing his movements or facial expressions or any kind of reaction. Therefore it was not accidental that when his eyes flashed at the chief's daughter, expressing a greedy desire for her, everybody, including the chief, noted the action with interest and curiosity. Some murmured, but the chief tried to be indifferent. He tried to be extrovert about his hospitality, "Well, my dear friend, I will grant you anything of your asking. If I trust my observation, there is something in your eyes which seems to be an expression of love for my daughter. Feel free to tell me your honest feelings because I will not deny you my daughter if it be your wish to have her. As a matter of fact, I will give her to you without your asking."

There was a great murmur in the crowd. The chief's daughter, Jiiko, had a reputation of being the most beautiful girl in the village. Yet she had such a modest reserve that people, especially young men, took her to be a proud, conceited egotist. There had been speculations of possible spouses, but none of them had ever come true. All the villagers had their eyes fixed onto Jiiko wondering what sort of man she would pick. Besides, she was the most valuable treasure in the chief's household. And when the chief indicated that he would part with his daughter, giving her to a stranger, the villagers confirmed that

Mulyankota must have magic powers. Otherwise how did he manage to get the fire from the rhino? And then the chief offered him his daughter! But Mulyankota exercised a high degree of caution.

"Your highness," he said, "I can't express in words how much your offer touches my heart. But, I am afraid, it is almost impossible for me to accept such an offer. As I have already mentioned, I would like to start on my journey back to my own village. And I suspect that you would not like to part with your daughter so unceremoniously; nor would you like her to go to a strange village which you know nothing about. Yet, I must start on my journey. I find I have to choose between two things: either to go back to my village and not marry your daughter, or marry your daughter and stay here. But since I am determined to go back to my home, I think it is most reasonable that I do not accept your offer."

The chief's reply surprised everybody: "Well, Mulyankota, you don't have to worry about staying here or not staying here. What does it matter whether you stay here or not? All that I want is the feeling that I have expressed my people's gratitude to you for having retrieved our fire. It will make me happy if I look back and say that I thanked you for your good deed. We people of Bwaya believe that gratitude and the expression of it, should be the foundation of human relationships. Therefore, I insist that I have to show you our gratitude for what you did for us. Since you do not deny that you desire my daughter, I offer her to you. Take her with you, wherever you want. I will feel satisfied because I know that I have done it as an expression of our gratitude. I will be even more satisfied to know that you have accepted our gratitude. So my final word is take my daughter with you."

No villager believed that their chief could do such a thing. Yet he did. And he offered to provide an escort as far as Mulyankota wanted. But Mulyankota turned down the offer for fear that the people escorting him might discover that he was a gourmand. Thus he left, just by himself and his newly acquired wife. They took a path down the valley into the thick forest. They never said a word to each other. As they entered the forest, Mulyankota began to recollect his experiences with the night-dancers. He began to fear going back home because of Nvannungi. He feared her. In any case he did not know the right path that would lead him back to his home village. He simply suspected that the path they took might be the right one.

In the forest, his mind became more and more restless. He became less and less aware of Jiiko's presence. He could no longer feel her; her pungent beauty was no longer noticeable. He felt as if he was seeing ghosts all around, and Jiiko one of the ghosts. He increased the pace in order to escape the ghostly forest. He seemed to move swiftly, swifter, in fact swifterest. He had never moved so swiftly in his life. Then he decided to run. If he ran hard enough, he probably would be able to escape those mysterious, invisible, ethereal ghosts haunting him. He wanted to escape from Jiiko. He wanted to escape to somewhere else. He no longer thought of home, nor of Jiiko, nor of Bwaya. He wanted a place where he could eat enough food, have enough sleep, and not be troubled by night-dancers. A place where nobody would take notice of him because he would be like every other person. He would be a member of the crowd, one of them. He wanted to be like every one else. So he ran hard trying to disentangle himself from the forest and from Jiiko. He wanted to be among people who could eat such amounts of food as he did.

Suddenly everything changed. No more forest, no more chief's daughter, no more running. He was exhausted. He discovered that he was in his home village, and Nvannungi came and took his hand, and in a commanding voice she said, "If you think you can ever run away from me, try again and you will see. I am everywhere. I am Nvannungi, but I am also Jiiko. When I possess, I don't let go. Now you are not only my husband, but in fact my subject. You're a cockroach, you will never get justice from a chicken; you are butter, you will never get justice from the sun; you are a white chicken, you will never hide from a kite."

MRS. PLUM

Ezekiel Mphahlele

South African Ezekiel Mphahlele, who has been
called the dean of African letters, is undoubtedly
the most versatile writer from Africa living today.
In addition to dozens of uncollected articles and
short stories, he is the author of *Down Second Avenue* (1959), an autobiographical account of his life
in South Africa; *The African Image* (1962), a pio-
neer volume of African literary criticism; *In Corner
B* (1967), a collection of short stories; and *The
Wanderers* (1970), a novel encompassing the entire
African continent. Dr. Mphahlele is currently teaching at the University of Denver. "Mrs. Plum" is
from *In Corner B*.

I

My madam's name was Mrs. Plum. She loved dogs and
Africans and said that everyone must follow the law even
if it hurt. These were three big things in Madam's life.

I came to work for Mrs. Plum in Greenside, not very
far from the center of Johannesburg, after leaving two
white families. The first white people I worked for as a
cook and laundry woman were a man and his wife in
Parktown North. They drank too much and always forgot
to pay me. After five months I said to myself No. I am
going to leave these drunks. So that was it. That day I
was as angry as a red-hot iron when it meets water. The
second house I cooked and washed for had five children
who were badly brought up. This was in Belgravia. Many
times they called me You Black Girl and I kept quiet.
Because their mother heard them and said nothing. Also

I was only new from Phokeng my home, far away near Rustenburg, I wanted to learn and know the white people before I knew how far to go with the others I would work for afterwards. The thing that drove me mad and made me pack and go was a man who came to visit them often. They said he was cousin or something like that. He came to the kitchen many times and tried to make me laugh. He patted me on the buttocks. I told the master. The man did it again and I asked the madam that very day to give me my money and let me go.

These were the first nine months after I had left Phokeng to work in Johannesburg. There were many of us girls and young women from Phokeng, from Zeerust, from Shuping, from Kosten, and many other places who came to work in the cities. So the suburbs were full of blackness. Most of us had already passed Standard Six and so we learned more English where we worked. None of us likes to work for white farmers, because we know too much about them on the farms near our homes. They do not pay well and they are cruel people.

At Easter time so many of us went home for a long weekend to see our people and to eat chicken and sour milk and *morogo*—wild spinach. We also took home sugar and condensed milk and tea and coffee and sweets and custard powder and tinned foods.

It was a home-girl of mine, Chimane, who called me to take a job in Mrs. Plum's house, just next door to where she worked. This is the third year now. I have been quite happy with Mrs. Plum and her daughter Kate. By this I mean that my place as a servant in Greenside is not as bad as that of many others. Chimane too does not complain much. We are paid six pounds a month with free food and free servant's room. No one can ever say that they are well paid, so we go on complaining somehow. Whenever we meet on Thursday afternoons, which is time off for all of us black women in the suburbs, we talk and talk and talk: about our people at home and their

letters; about their illnesses; about bad crops; about a sister
who wanted a school uniform and books and school fees;
about some of our madams and masters who are good, or
stingy with money or food, or stupid or full of nonsense,
or who kill themselves and each other, or who are dirty
—and so many things I cannot count them all.

Thursday afternoons we go to town to look at the shops,
to attend a woman's club, to see our boy friends, to go to
bioscope some of us. We turn up smart, to show others
the clothes we bought from the black men who sell soft
goods to servants in the suburbs. We take a number of
things and they come round every month for a bit of
money until we finish paying. Then we dress the way of
many white madams and girls. I think we look really
smart. Sometimes we catch the eyes of a white woman
looking at us and we laugh and laugh until we nearly drop
on the ground because we feel good inside ourselves.

II

What did the girl next door call you? Mrs. Plum asked
me the first day I came to her. Jane, I replied. Was there
not an African name? I said yes, Karabo. All right, Madam
said. We'll call you Karabo, she said. She spoke as if she
knew a name is a big thing. I knew so many whites who
did not care what they called black people as long as it was
all right for their tongue. This pleased me, I mean Mrs.
Plum's use of *Karabo*; because the only time I heard the
name was when I was home or when my friends spoke
to me. Then she showed me what to do: meals, meal
times, washing, and where all the things were that I was
going to use.

My daughter will be here in the evening, Madam said.
She is at school. When the daughter came, she added, she
would tell me some of the things she wanted me to do for
her every day.

Chimane, my friend next door, had told me about the

daughter Kate, how wild she seemed to be, and about Mr. Plum who had killed himself with a gun in a house down the street. They had left the house and come to this one.

Madam is a tall woman. Not slender, not fat. She moves slowly, and speaks slowly. Her face looks very wise, her forehead seems to tell me she has a strong liver: she is not afraid of anything. Her eyes are always swollen at the lower eyelids like a white person who has not slept for many many nights or like a large frog. Perhaps it is because she smokes too much, like wet wood that will not know whether to go up in flames or stop burning. She looks me straight in the eyes when she talks to me, and I know she does this with other people too. At first this made me fear her, now I am used to her. She is not a lazy woman, and she does many things outside, in the city and in the suburbs.

This was the first thing her daughter Kate told me when she came and we met. Don't mind mother, Kate told me. She said, She is sometimes mad with people for very small things. She will soon be all right and speak nicely to you again.

Kate, I like her very much, and she likes me too. She tells me many things a white woman does not tell a black servant. I mean things about what she likes and does not like, what her mother does or does not do, all these. At first I was unhappy and wanted to stop her, but now I do not mind.

Kate looks very much like her mother in the face. I think her shoulders will be just as round and strong-looking. She moves faster than Madam. I asked her why she was still at school when she was so big. She laughed. Then she tried to tell me that the school where she was was for big people, who had finished with lower school. She was learning big things about cooking and food. She can explain better, me I cannot. She came home on week-ends.

Since I came to work for Mrs. Plum Kate has been

teaching me plenty of cooking. I first learned from her and Madam the word *recipes*. When Kate was at the big school, Madam taught me how to read cookery books. I went on very slowly at first, slower than an ox-wagon. Now I know more. When Kate came home, she found I had read the recipe she left me. So we just cooked straight-away. Kate thinks I am fit to cook in a hotel. Madam thinks so too. Never never! I thought. Cooking in a hotel is like feeding oxen. No one can say thank you to you. After a few months I could cook the Sunday lunch and later I could cook specials for Madam's or Kate's guests.

Madam did not only teach me cooking. She taught me how to look after guests. She praised me when I did very very well; not like the white people I had worked for before. I do not know what runs crooked in the heads of other people. Madam also had classes in the evenings for servants to teach them how to read and write. She and two other women in Greenside taught in a church hall.

As I say, Kate tells me plenty of things about Madam. She says to me she says, My mother goes to meetings many times. I ask her I say, What for? She says to me she says, For your people. I ask her I say, My people are in Phokeng far away. They have got mouths, I say. Why does she want to say something for them? Does she know what my mother and what my father want to say? They can speak when they want to. Kate raises her shoulders and drops them and says, How can I tell you Karabo? I don't say your people—your family only. I mean all the black people in this country. I say Oh! What do the black people want to say? Again she raises her shoulders and drops them, taking a deep breath.

I ask her I say, With whom is she in the meeting?

She says, With other people who think like her.

I ask her I say, Do you say there are people in the world who think the same things?

She nods her head.

I ask, What things?

So that a few of your people should one day be among those who rule this country, get more money for what they do for the white man, and—what did Kate say again? Yes, that Madam and those who think like her also wanted my people who have been to school to choose those who must speak for them in the—I think she said it looks like a *Kgotla* at home who rule the villages.

I say to Kate I say, Oh I see now. I say, Tell me Kate why is madam always writing on the machine, all the time everyday nearly?

She replies she says, Oh my mother is writing books.

I ask, You mean a book like those?—pointing at the books on the shelves.

Yes, Kate says.

And she told me how Madam wrote books and other things for newspapers and she wrote for the newspapers and magazines to say things for the black people who should be treated well, be paid more money, for the black people who can read and write many things to choose those who want to speak for them.

Kate also told me she said, My mother and other women who think like her put on black belts over their shoulders when they are sad and they want to show the white government they do not like the things being done by whites to blacks. My mother and the others go and stand where the people in government are going to enter or go out of a building.

I ask her I say, Does the government and the white people listen and stop their sins? She says No. But my mother is in another group of white people.

I ask, Do the people of the government give the women tea and cakes? Kate says, Karabo! How stupid; oh!

I say to her I say, Among my people if someone comes and stands in front of my house I tell him to come in and I give him food. You white people are wonderful. But they keep standing there and the government people do not give them anything.

She replies, You mean strange. How many times have I taught you not to say *wonderful* when you mean *strange!* Well, Kate says with a short heart and looking cross and she shouts, Well they do not stand there the whole day to ask for tea and cakes stupid. Oh dear!

Always when Madam finished to read her newspapers she gave them to me to read to help me speak and write better English. When I had read she asked me to tell her some of the things in it. In this way, I did better and better and my mind was opening and opening and I was learning and learning many things about the black people inside and outside the towns which I did not know in the least. When I found words that were too difficult or I did not understand some of the things I asked Madam. She always told me You see this, you see that, eh? with a heart that can carry on a long way. Yes, Madam writes many letters to the papers. She is always sore about the way the white police beat up black people; about the way black people who work for whites are made to sit at the Zoo Lake with their hearts hanging, because the white people say our people are making noise on Sunday afternoon when they want to rest in their houses and gardens; about many ugly things that happen when some white people meet black man on the pavement or street. So Madam writes to the papers to let others know, to ask the government to be kind to us.

In the first year Mrs. Plum wanted me to eat at table with her. It was very hard, one because I was not used to eating at table with a fork and knife, two because I heard of no other kitchen worker who was handled like this. I was afraid. Afraid of everybody, of Madam's guests if they found me doing this. Madam said I must not be silly. I must show that African servants can also eat at table. Number three, I could not eat some of the things I loved very much: mealie-meal porridge with sour milk or *morogo*, stamped mealies mixed with butter beans, sour porridge for breakfast and other things. Also, except for morning porridge, our food is nice when you eat with the hand. So nice that it does not stop in the mouth or the throat to greet anyone before it passes smoothly down.

We often had lunch together with Chimane next door and our garden boy—Ha! I must remember never to say *boy* again when I talk about a man. This makes me think of a day during the first few weeks in Mrs. Plum's house. I was talking about Dick her garden man and I said "garden boy." And she says to me she says, Stop talking about a "boy," Karabo. Now listen here, she says, You Africans must learn to speak properly about each other. And she says White people won't talk kindly about you if you look down upon each other.

I say to her I say Madam, I learned the word from the white people I worked for, and all the kitchen maids say "boy."

She replies she says to me, Those are white people who know nothing, just low-class whites. I say to her I say I thought white people know everything.

She said, You'll learn, my girl, and you must start in this house, hear? She left me there thinking, my mind mixed up.

I learned. I grew up.

III

If any woman or girl does not know the Black Crow Club in Bree Street, she does not know anything. I think nearly everything takes place inside and outside that house. It is just where the dirty part of the City begins, with factories and the market. After the market is the place where Indians and Colored people live. It is also at the Black Crow that the buses turn round and back to the black townships. Noise, noise, noise all the time. There are woman who sell hot sweet potatoes and fruit and monkey nuts and boiled eggs in the winter, boiled mealies and the other things in the summer, all these on the pavements. The streets are always full of potato and fruit skins

and monkey nut shells. There is always a strong smell of
roast pork. I think it is because of Piel's cold storage down
Bree Street.

Madam said she knew the black people who work in
the Black Crow. She was happy that I was spending my
afternoon on Thursday in such a club. You will learn
sewing, knitting, she said, and other things that you like.
Do you like to dance? I told her I said, Yes, I want to
learn. She paid the two shillings fee for me each month.

We waited on the first floor, we the ones who were
learning sewing; waiting for the teacher. We talked and
laughed about madams and masters, and their children
and their dogs and birds and whispered about our boy
friends.

Sies! My Madam you do not know—*mojuta od'nete*—
a real miser . . .

Jo—jo—jo! you should see our new dog. A big thing
like this. People! Big in a foolish way . . .

What! Me, I take a master's bitch by the leg, me, and
throw it away so that it keeps howling, *tjwe—tjwe! ngo—
wu ngo—wu!* I don't play about with them, me . . .

Shame, poor thing! God sees you, true. . . !

They wanted me to take their dog out for a walk every
afternoon and I told them I said It is not my work in
other houses the garden man does it. I just said to myself
I said they can go to the chickens. Let them bite their
elbow before I take out a dog, I am not so mad yet . . .

Hei! It is not like the child of my white people who
keeps a big white rat and you know what? He puts in on
his bed when he goes to school. And let the blankets just
begin to smell of urine and all the nonsense and they tell
me to wash them. *Hei*, people . . . !

Did you hear about Rebone, people? Her Madam put
her out, because her master was always tapping her buttocks with his fingers. And yesterday the madam saw the
master press Rebone against himself . . .

Jo—jo—jo! people. . . !

Dirty white man!

No, not dirty. The madam smells too old for him.

Hei! Go and wash your mouth with soap, this girl's mouth is dirty . . .

Jo, Rebone, daughter of the people! We must help her to find a job before she thinks of going back home.

The teacher came. A woman with strong legs, a strong face, and kind eyes. She had short hair and dressed in a simple but lovely floral frock. She stood well on her legs and hips. She had a black mark between the two top front teeth. She smiled as if we were her children. Our group began with games, and then Lilian Ngoyi took us for sewing. After this she gave a brief talk to all of us from the different classes.

I can never forget the things this woman said and how she put them to us. She told us that the time had passed for black girls and women in the suburbs to be satisfied with working, sending money to our people and going to see them once a year. We were to learn, she said, that the world would never be safe for black people until they were in the government with the power to make laws. The power should be given by the Africans who were more than the whites.

We asked her questions and she answered them with wisdom. I shall put some of them down in my own words as I remember them.

Shall we take the place of the white people in the government?

Some yes. But we shall be more than they as we are more in the country. But also the people of all colours will come together and there are good white men we can choose and there are Africans some white people will choose to be in the government.

There are good madams and masters and bad ones. Should we take the good ones for friends?

A master and a servant can never be friends. Never, so put that out of your head, will you! You are not even sure if the ones you say are good are not like that because they cannot breathe or live without the work of your hands.

As long as you need their money, face them with respect. But you must know that many sad things are happening in our country and you, all of you, must always be learning, adding to what you already know, and obey us when we ask you to help us.

At other times Lilian Ngoyi told us she said, Remember your poor people at home and the way in which the whites are moving them from place to place like sheep and cattle. And at other times again she told us she said, Remember that a hand cannot wash itself, it needs another to do it.

I always thought of Madam when Lilian Ngoyi spoke. I asked myself, What would she say if she knew that I was listening to such words. Words like: A white man is looked after by his black nanny and his mother when he is a baby. When he grows up the white government looks after him, sends him to school, makes it impossible for him to suffer from the great hunger, keeps a job ready and open for him as soon as he wants to leave school. Now Lilian Ngoyi asked she said, How many white people can be born in a white hospital, grow up in white streets, be clothed in lovely cotton, lie on white cushions; how many whites can live all their lives in a fenced place away from people of other colours and then, as men and women learn quickly the correct ways of thinking, learn quickly to ask questions in their minds, big questions that will throw over all the nice things of a white man's life? How many? Very very few! For those whites who have not begun to ask, it is too late. For those who have begun and are joining us with both feet in our house, we can only say Welcome!

I was learning. I was growing up. Every time I thought of Madam, she became more and more like a dark forest which one fears to enter, and which one will never know. But there were several times when I thought, This woman is easy to understand, she is like all other white women.

What else are they teaching you at the Black Crow, Karabo?

I tell her I say, nothing, Madam. I ask her I say Why does Madam ask?

You are changing.

What does Madam mean?

Well, you are changing.

But we are always changing Madam.

And she left me standing in the kitchen. This was a few days after I had told her that I did not want to read more than one white paper a day. The only magazines I wanted to read, I said to her, were those from overseas, if she had them. I told her that white papers had pictures of white people most of the time. They talked mostly about white people and their gardens, dogs, weddings and parties. I asked her if she could buy me a Sunday paper that spoke about my people. Madam bought it for me. I did not think she would do it.

There were mornings when, after hanging the white people's washing on the line Chimane and I stole a little time to stand at the fence and talk. We always stood where we could be hidden by our rooms.

Hei, Karabo, you know what? That was Chimane.

No—what? Before you start, tell me, has Timi come back to you?

Ach, I do not care. He is still angry. But boys are fools they always come back dragging themselves on their empty bellies. *Hei* you know what?

Yes?

The Thursday past I saw Moruti K.K. I laughed until I dropped on the ground. He is standing in front of the Black Crow. I believe his big stomach was crying from hunger. Now he has a small dog in his armpit, and is standing before a woman selling boiled eggs and—*hei* home-girl!—tripe and intestines are boiling in a pot—oh —the smell! you could fill a hungry belly with it, the way it was good. I think Moruti K.K. is waiting for the woman to buy a boiled egg. I do not know what the woman was still doing. I am standing nearby. The dog keeps wriggling and pushing out its nose, looking at the boiling tripe. Moruti keeps patting it with his free hand, not so? Again the dog wants to spill out of Moruti's hand and it gives a few sounds through the nose. *Hei* man, home-girl! One two three the dog spills out to catch some of the good meat! It misses falling into the hot gravy in which the tripe is swimming I do not know how. Moruti K.K. tries to chase it. It has tumbled on to the women's eggs and potatoes and all are in the dust. She stands up and goes after K.K. She is shouting to him to pay, not so? Where am I at that time? I am nearly dead with laughter the tears are coming down so far.

I was myself holding tight on the fence so as not to fall through laughing. I held my stomach to keep back a pain in the side.

I ask her I say, Did Moruti K.K. come back to pay for the wasted food?

Yes, he paid.

The dog?

He caught it. That is a good African dog. A dog must look for its own food when it is not time for meals. Not these stupid spoiled angels the whites keep giving tea and biscuits.

Hmm.

Dick our garden man joined us, as he often did. When the story was repeated to him the man nearly rolled on the ground laughing.

He asks who is Reverend K.K.?

I say he is the owner of the Black Crow.

Oh!

We reminded each other, Chimane and I, of the round minister. He would come into the club, look at us with a smooth smile on his smooth round face. He would look at each one of us, with that smile on all the time, as if he had forgotten that it was there. Perhaps he had, because as he looked at us, almost stripping us naked with his watery shining eyes—funny—he could have been a farmer looking at his ripe corn, thinking many things.

K.K. often spoke without shame about what he called

ripe girls—*matjitjana*—with good firm breasts. He said such girls were pure without any nonsense in their heads and bodies. Everybody talked a great deal about him and what they thought he must be doing in his office whenever he called in so-and-so.

The Reverend K.K. did not belong to any church. He baptised, married, and buried people for a fee, who had no church to do such things for them. They said he had been driven out of the Presbyterian Church. He had formed his own, but it did not go far. Then he later came and opened the Black Crow. He knew just how far to go with Lilian Ngoyi. She said although she used his club to teach us things that would help us in life, she could not go on if he was doing any wicked things with the girls in his office. Moruti K.K. feared her, and kept his place.

IV

When I began to tell my story I thought I was going to tell you mostly about Mrs. Plum's two dogs. But I have been talking about people. I think Dick is right when he says What is a dog! And there are so many dogs cats and parrots in Greenside and other places that Mrs. Plum's dogs do not look special. But there was something special in the dog business in Madam's house. The way in which she loved them, maybe.

Monty is a tiny animal with long hair and small black eyes and a face nearly like that of an old woman. The other, Malan, is a bit bigger, with brown and white colors. It has small hair and looks naked by the side of the friend. They sleep in two separate baskets which stay in Madam's bedroom. They are to be washed often and brushed and sprayed and they sleep on pink linen. Monty has a pink ribbon which stays on his neck most of the time. They both carry a cover on their backs. They make me fed up when I see them in their baskets, looking fat, and as if they knew all that was going on everywhere.

It was Dick's work to look after Monty and Malan, to

feed them, and to do everything for them. He did this together with garden work and cleaning of the house. He came at the beginning of this year. He just came, as if from nowhere, and Madam gave him the job as she had chased away two before him, she told me. In both those cases, she said that they could not look after Monty and Malan.

Dick had a long heart, even although he told me and Chimane that European dogs were stupid, spoiled. He said One day those white people will put ear rings and toe rings and bangles on their dogs. That would be the day he would leave Mrs. Plum. For, he said, he was sure that she would want him to polish the rings and bangles with Brasso.

Although he had a long heart, Madam was still not sure of him. She often went to the dogs after a meal or after a cleaning and said to them Did Dick give you food sweethearts? Or, Did Dick wash you sweethearts? Let me see. And I could see that Dick was blowing up like a balloon with anger. These things called white people! he said to me. Talking to dogs!

I say to him I say, People talk to oxen at home do I not say so?

Yes, he says, but at home do you not know that a man speaks to an ox because he wants to make it pull the plow or the wagon or to stop or to stand still for a person to inspan it. No one simply goes to an ox looking at him with eyes far apart and speaks to it. Let me ask you, do you ever see a person where we come from take a cow and press it to his stomach or his cheek? Tell me!

And I say to Dick I say, We were talking about an ox, not a cow.

He laughed with his broad mouth until tears came out of his eyes. At a certain point I laughed aloud too.

One day when you have time, Dick says to me, he says, you should look into Madam's bedroom when she has put a notice outside her door.

Dick, what are you saying? I ask.

I do not talk, me. I know deep inside me.

Dick was about our age, I and Chimane. So we always said *moshiman'o* when we spoke about his tricks. Because he was not too big to be a boy to us. He also said to us *Hei, lona banyana kelona*—Hey you girls, you! His large mouth always seemed to be making ready to laugh. I think Madam did not like this. Many times she would say What is there to make you laugh here? Or in the garden she would say This is a flower and when it wants water that is not funny! Or again, if you did more work and stopped trying to water my plants with your smile you would be more useful. Even when Dick did not mean to smile. What Madam did not get tired of saying was, If I left you to look after my dogs without anyone to look after you at the same time you would drown the poor things.

Dick smiled at Mrs. Plum. Dick hurt Mrs. Plum's dogs? Then cows can fly. He was really—really afraid of white people, Dick. I think he tried very hard not to feel afraid. For he was always showing me and Chimane in private how Mrs. Plum walked, and spoke. He took two bowls and pressed them to his chest, speaking softly to them as Madam speaks to Monty and Malan. Or he sat at Madam's table and acted the way she sits when writing. Now and again he looked back over his shoulder, pulled his face long like a horse's making as if he were looking over his glasses while telling me something to do. Then he would sit on one of the armchairs, cross his legs and act the way Madam drank her tea; he held the cup he was thinking about between his thumb and the pointing finger, only letting their nails meet. And he laughed after every act. He did these things, of course, when Madam was not home. And where was I at such times? Almost flat on my stomach, laughing.

But oh how Dick trembled when Mrs. Plum scolded him! He did his house-cleaning very well. Whatever mistake he made, it was mostly with the dogs; their linen, their food. One white man came into the house one afternoon to tell Madam that Dick had been very careless when taking the dogs out for a walk. His own dog was waiting on Madam's stoop. He repeated that he had been driving down our street; and Dick had let loose Monty and Malan to cross the street. The white man made plenty of noise about this and I think wanted to let Madam know how useful he had been. He kept on saying Just one inch, *just* one inch. It was lucky I put on my brakes quick enough. . . . But your boy kept on smiling— Why? Strange. My boy would only do it twice and only twice and then. . . ! His pass. The man moved his hand like one writing, to mean that he would sign his servant's pass for him to go and never come back. When he left, the white man said Come on Rusty, the boy is waiting to clean you. Dogs with names, men without, I thought.

Madam climbed on top of Dick for this, as we say.

Once one of the dogs, I don't know which—Malan or Monty—took my stocking—brand new, you hear—and tore it with its teeth and paws. When I told Madam about it, my anger as high as my throat, she gave me money to buy another pair. It happened again. This time she said she was not going to give me money because I must also keep my stockings where the two gentlemen would not reach them. Mrs. Plum did not want us ever to say *Voetsek* when we wanted the dogs to go away. Me I said this when they came sniffing at my legs or fingers. I hate it.

In my third year in Mrs. Plum's house, many things happened, most of them all bad for her. There was trouble with Kate; Chimane had big trouble; my heart was twisted by two loves; and Monty and Malan became real dogs for a few days.

Madam had a number of suppers and parties. She invited Africans to some of them. Kate told me the reasons for some of the parties. Like her mother's books when finished, a visitor from across the seas and so on. I did not like the black people who came here to drink and eat. They spoke such difficult English like people who were full of all the books in the world. They looked at me as if I were right down there whom they thought little of —me a black person like them.

One day I heard Kate speak to her mother. She says I don't know why you ask so many Africans to the house. A few will do at a time. She said something about the government which I could not hear well. Madam replies she says to her You know some of them do not meet white people often, so far away in their dark houses. And she says to Kate that they do not come because they want her as a friend but they just want a drink for nothing.

I simply felt that I could not be the servant of white people and of blacks at the same time. At my home or in my room I could serve them without a feeling of shame. And now, if they were only coming to drink!

But one of the black men and his sister always came to the kitchen to talk to me. I must have looked unfriendly the first time, for Kate talked to me about it afterwards as she was in the kitchen when they came. I know that at that time I was not easy at all. I was ashamed and I felt that a white person's house was not the place for me to look happy in front of other black people while the white man looked on.

Another time it was easier. The man was alone. I shall never forget that night, as long as I live. He spoke kind words and I felt my heart grow big inside me. It caused me to tremble. There were several other visits. I knew that I loved him, I could never know what he really thought of me, I mean as a woman and he as a man. But I loved him, and I still think of him with a sore heart. Slowly I came to know the pain of it. Because he was a doctor and so full of knowledge and English I could not reach him. So I knew he could not stoop down to see me as someone who wanted him to love me.

Kate turned very wild. Mrs. Plum was very much worried. Suddenly it looked as if she were a new person, with new ways and new everything. I do not know what was wrong or right. She began to play the big gramophone aloud, as if the music were for the whole of Greenside. The music was wild and she twisted her waist all the time, with her mouth half-open. She did the same things in her room. She left the big school and every Saturday night now she went out. When I looked at her face, there was something deep and wild there on it, and when I thought she looked young she looked old, and when I thought she looked old she was young. We were both 22 years of age. I think that I could see the reason why her mother was so worried, why she was suffering.

Worse was to come.

They were now openly screaming at each other. They began in the sitting room and went upstairs together, speaking fast hot biting words, some of which I did not grasp. One day Madam comes to me and says You know Kate loves an African, you know the doctor who comes to supper here often. She says he loves her too and they will leave the country and marry outside. Tell me, Karabo, what do your people think of this kind of thing between a white woman and a black man? It *cannot* be right is it?

I reply and I say to her We have never seen it happen before where I come from.

That's right, Karabo, it is just madness.

Madam left. She looked like a hunted person.

These white women, I say to myself I say these white women, why do not they love their own men and leave us to love ours!

From that minute I knew that I would never want to speak to Kate. She appeared to me as a thief, as a fox that falls upon a flock of sheep at night. I hated her. To make it worse, he would never be allowed to come to the house again.

Whenever she was home there was silence between us. I no longer wanted to know anything about what she was doing, where or how.

I lay awake for hours on my bed. Lying like that, I seemed to feel parts of my body beat and throb inside me, the way I have seen big machines doing, pounding and pounding and pushing and pulling and pouring some water into one hole which came out at another end. I stretched myself so many times so as to feel tired and sleepy.

When I did sleep, my dreams were full of painful things.

One evening I made up my mind, after putting it off many times. I told my boy-friend that I did not want him any longer. He looked hurt, and that hurt me too. He left.

The thought of the African doctor was still with me and it pained me to know that I should never see him again; unless I met him in the street on a Thursday afternoon. But he had a car. Even if I did meet him by luck, how could I make him see that I loved him? Ach, I do not believe he would even stop to think what kind of woman I am. Part of that winter was a time of longing and burning for me. I say part because there are always things to keep servants busy whose white people go to the sea for the winter.

To tell the truth, winter was the time for servants; not nannies, because they went with their madams so as to look after the children. Those like me stayed behind to look after the house and dogs. In winter so many families went away that the dogs remained the masters and madams. You could see them walk like white people in the streets. Silent but with plenty of power. And when you saw them you knew that they were full of more nonsense and fancies in the house.

There was so little work to do.

One week word was whispered round that a home-boy of ours was going to hold a party in his room on Saturday. I think we all took it for a joke. How could the man be so bold and stupid? The police were always driving about at night looking for black people; and if the whites next door heard the party noise—*oho!* But still, we were full of joy and wanted to go. As for Dick, he opened his big mouth and nearly fainted when he heard of it and that I was really going.

During the day on the big Saturday Kate came.

She seemed a little less wild. But I was not ready to talk to her. I was surprised to hear myself answer her when she said to me Mother says you do not like a marriage between a white girl and a black man, Karabo.

Then she was silent.

She says But I want to help him, Karabo.

I ask her I say You want to help him to do what?

To go higher and higher, to the top.

I knew I wanted to say so much that was boiling in my chest. I could not say it. I thought of Lilian Ngoyi at the Black Crow, what she said to us. But I was mixed up in my head and in my blood.

You still agree with my mother?

All I could say was I said to your mother I had never seen a black man and a white woman marrying, you hear me? What I think about it is my business.

I remembered that I wanted to iron my party dress and so I left her. My mind was full of the party again and I was glad because Kate and the doctor would not worry my peace that day. And the next day the sun would shine for all of us, Kate or no Kate, doctor or no doctor.

The house where our home-boy worked was hidden from the main road by a number of trees. But although we asked a number of questions and counted many fingers of bad luck until we had no more hands for fingers, we put on our best pay-while-you-wear dresses and suits and clothes bought from boys who had stolen them, and went to our home-boy's party. We whispered all the way while we climbed up to the house. Someone who knew told us that the white people next door were away for the winter. Oh, so that is the thing! we said.

We poured into the garden through the back and stood in front of his room laughing quietly. He came from the big house behind us, and were we not struck dumb when he told us to go into the white people's house! Was he mad? We walked in with slow footsteps that seemed to be sniffing at the floor, not sure of anything. Soon we were standing and sitting all over on the nice warm cushions and the heaters were on. Our home-boy turned the lights low. I counted fifteen people inside. We saw how we loved one another's evening dress. The boys were smart too.

Our home-boy's girl-friend Naomi was busy in the kitchen preparing food. He took out glasses and cold drinks—fruit juice, tomato juice, ginger beers, and so many other kinds of soft drink. It was just too nice. The tarts, the biscuits, the snacks, the cakes, woo, that was a party, I tell you. I think I ate more ginger cake than I had ever done in my life. Naomi had baked some of the things. Our home-boy came to me and said I do not want the police to come here and have reason to arrest us, so I am not serving hot drinks, not even beer. There is no law that we cannot have parties, is there? So we can feel free. Our use of this house is the master's business. If I had asked him he would have thought me mad.

I say to him I say, You have a strong liver to do such a thing.

He laughed.

He played pennywhistle music on gramophone records —Miriam Makeba, Dorothy Masuka, and other African singers and players. We danced and the party became more and more noisy and more happy. Hai, those girls Miriam and Dorothy, they can sing, I tell you! We ate more and laughed more and told more stories. In the middle of the party, our home-boy called us to listen to what he was going to say. Then he told us how he and a friend of his in Orlando collected money to bet on a horse for the July Handicap in Durban. They did this each year but lost. Now they had won two hundred pounds. We all clapped hands and cheered. Two hundred pounds woo!

You should go and sit at home and just eat time, I say to him. He laughs and says You have no understanding not one little bit.

To all of us he says Now my brothers and sisters enjoy

yourselves. At home I should slaughter a goat for us to feast and thank our ancestors. But this is town life and we must thank them with tea and cake and all those sweet things. I know some people think I must be so bold that I could be midwife to a lion that is giving birth, but enjoy yourselves and have no fear.

Madam came back looking strong and fresh.

The very week she arrived the police had begun again to search servants' rooms. They were looking for what they called loafers and men without passes who they said were living with friends in the suburbs against the law. Our dog's-meat boys became scarce because of the police. A boy who had a girl-friend in the kitchens, as we say, always told his friends that he was coming for dog's meat when he meant he was visiting his girl. This was because we gave our boy-friends part of the meat the white people bought for the dogs and us.

One night a white and a black policeman entered Mrs. Plum's yard. They said they had come to search. She says no, they cannot. They say Yes, they must do it. She answers No. They forced their way to the back, to Dick's room and mine. Mrs. Plum took the hose that was running in the front garden and quickly went round to the back. I cut across the floor to see what she was going to say to the men. They were talking to Dick, using dirty words. Mrs. Plum did not wait, she just pointed the hose at the two policemen. This seemed to surprise them. They turned round and she pointed it into their faces. Without their seeing me I went to the tap at the corner of the house and opened it more. I could see Dick, like me, was trying to keep down his laughter. They shouted and tried to wave the water away, but she kept the hose pointing at them, now moving it up and down. They turned and ran through the back gate, swearing the while.

That fixes them, Mrs. Plum said.

The next day the morning paper reported it.

They arrived in the afternoon—the two policemen—with another. They pointed out Mrs. Plum and she was led to the police station. They took her away to answer for stopping the police while they were doing their work.

She came back and said she had paid bail.

At the magistrate's court, Madam was told that she had done a bad thing. She would have to pay a fine or else go to prison for fourteen days. She said she would go to jail to show that she felt she was not in the wrong.

Kate came and tried to tell her that she was doing something silly going to jail for a small thing like that. She tells Madam she says This is not even a thing to take to the high court. Pay the money. What is £5?

Madam went to jail.

She looked very sad when she came out. I thought of what Lilian Ngoyi often said to us: You must be ready to go to jail for the things you believe are true and for which you are taken by the police. What did Mrs. Plum really believe about me, Chimane, Dick, and all the other black people? I asked myself. I did not know. But from all those things she was writing for the papers and all those meetings she was going to where white people talked about black people and the way they are treated by the government, from what those white women with black bands over their shoulders were doing standing where a white government man was going to pass, I said to myself I said This woman, *hai*, I do not know she seems to think very much of us black people. But why was she so sad?

Kate came back home to stay after this. She still played the big gramophone loud-loud-loud and twisted her body at her waist until I thought it was going to break. Then I saw a young white man come often to see her. I watched them through the opening near the hinges of the door between the kitchen and the sitting room where they sat. I saw them kiss each other for a long time. I saw him lift up Kate's dress and her white-white legs begin to tremble, and—oh I am afraid to say more, my heart was beating hard. She called him Jim. I thought it was funny because white people in the shops call black men Jim.

Kate had begun to play with Jim when I met a boy

who loved me and I loved. He was much stronger than
the one I sent away and I loved him more, much more.
The face of the doctor came to my mind often, but it did
not hurt me so any more. I stopped looking at Kate and
her Jim through openings. We spoke to each other, Kate
and I, almost as freely as before but not quite. She and
her mother were friends again.

Hallo, Karabo, I heard Chimane call me one morning
as I was starching my apron. I answered. I went to the
line to hang it. I saw she was standing at the fence, so I
knew she had something to tell me. I went to her.

Hallo!

Hallo, Chimane!

O *kae?*

Ke teng. Wena?

At that moment a woman came out through the back
door of the house where Chimane was working.

I have not seen that one before, I say, pointing with
my head.

Chimane looked back. Oh, that one. *Hei*, daughter-of-
the-people, *Hei*, you have not seen miracles. You know
this is Madam's mother-in-law as you see her there. Did I
never tell you about her?

No, never.

White people, nonsense. You know what? That poor
woman is here now for two days. She has to cook for
herself and I cook for the family.

On the same stove?

Yes, She comes after me when I have finished.

She has her own food to cook?

Yes, Karabo. White people have no heart no sense.

What will eat them up if they share their food?

Ask me, just ask me. God! She clapped her hands to
show that only God knew, and it was His business, not
ours.

Chimane asks me she says, Have you heard from home?

I tell her I say, Oh daughter-of-the-people, more and
more deaths. Something is finishing the people at home.

My mother has written. She says they are all right, my father too and my sisters, except for the people who have died. Malebo, the one who lived alone in the house I showed you last year, a white house, he is gone. Then teacher Sedimo. He was very thin and looked sick all the time. He taught my sisters not me. His mother-in-law you remember I told you died last year—no, the year before. Mother says also there is a woman she does not think I remember because I last saw her when I was a small girl she passed away in Zeerust she was my mother's greatest friend when they were girls. She would have gone to her burial if it was not because she has swollen feet.

How are the feet?

She says they are still giving her trouble. I ask Chimane, How are your people at Nokaneng? They have not written?

She shook her head.

I could see from her eyes that her mind was on another thing and not her people at that moment.

Wait for me Chimane eh, forgive me, I have scones in the oven, eh! I will just take them out and come back, eh!

When I came back to her Chimane was wiping her eyes. They were wet.

Karabo, you know what?

E—e. I shook my head.

I am heavy with child.

Hau!

There was a moment of silence.

Who is it, Chimane?

Timi. He came back only to give me this.

But he loves you. What does he say have you told him?

I told him yesterday. We met in town.

I remembered I had not seen her at the Black Crow. Are you sure, Chimane? You have missed a month?

She nodded her head.

Timi himself—he did not use the thing?

I only saw after he finished, that he had not.

Why? What does he say?

He tells me he says I should not worry I can be his wife.

Timi is a good boy, Chimane. How many of these boys with town ways who know too much will even say Yes it is my child?

Hai, Karabo, you are telling me other things now. Do you not see that I have not worked long enough for my people? If I marry now who will look after them when I am the only child?

Hm. I hear your words. It is true. I tried to think of something soothing to say.

Then I say You can talk it over with Timi. You can go home and when the child is born you look after it for three months and when you are married you come to town to work and can put your money together to help the old people while they are looking after the child.

What shall we be eating all the time I am at home? It is not like those days gone past when we had land and our mother could go to the fields until the child was ready to arrive.

The light goes out in my mind and I cannot think of the right answer. How many times have I feared the same thing! Luck and the mercy of the gods that is all I live by. That is all we live by—all of us.

Listen, Karabo. I must be going to make tea for Madam. It will soon strike half-past ten.

I went back to the house. As Madam was not in yet, I threw myself on the divan in the sitting-room. Malan came sniffing at my legs. I put my foot under its fat belly and shoved it up and away from me so that it cried *tjunk —tjunk—tjunk* as it went out. I say to it I say Go and tell your brother what I have done to you and tell him to try it and see what I will do. Tell your grandmother when she comes home too.

When I lifted my eyes he was standing in the kitchen door, Dick. He says to me he says *Hau!* now you have also begun to speak to dogs!

I did not reply. I just looked at him, his mouth ever

stretched out like the mouth of a bag, and I passed to my room.

I sat on my bed and looked at my face in the mirror. Since the morning I had been feeling as if a black cloud were hanging over me, pressing on my head and shoulders. I do not know how long I sat there. Then I smelled Madam. What was it? Where was she? After a few moments I knew what it was. My perfume and scent. I used the same cosmetics as Mrs. Plum's. I should have been used to it by now. But this morning—why did I smell Mrs. Plum like this? Then, without knowing why, I asked myself I said, Why have I been using the same cosmetics as Madam? I wanted to throw them all out. I stopped. And then I took all the things and threw them into the dustbin. I was going to buy other kinds on Thursday; finished!

I could not sit down. I went out and into the white people's house. I walked through and the smell of the house made me sick and seemed to fill up my throat. I went to the bathroom without knowing why. It was full of the smell of Madam. Dick was cleaning the bath. I stood at the door and looked at him cleaning the dirt out of the bath, dirt from Madam's body. *Sies!* I said aloud. To myself I said, Why cannot people wash the dirt of their own bodies out of the bath? Before Dick knew I was near I went out. Ach, I said again to myself, why should I think about it now when I have been doing their washing for so long and cleaned the bath many times when Dick was ill. I had held worse things from her body times without number . . .

I went out and stood midway between the house and my room, looking into the next yard. The three-legged grey cat next door came to the fence and our eyes met. I do not know how long we stood like that looking at each other. I was thinking, Why don't you go and look at your grandmother like that? when it turned away and mewed hopping on the three legs. Just like someone who feels pity for you.

In my room I looked into the mirror on the chest of drawers. I thought Is this Karabo this?

Thursday came, and the afternoon off. At the Black Crow I did not see Chimane. I wondered about her. In the evening I found a note under my door. It told me if Chimane was not back that evening I should know that she was at 660 3rd Avenue, Alexandra Township. I was not to tell the white people.

I asked Dick if he could not go to Alexandra with me after I had washed the dishes. At first he was unwilling. But I said to him I said, Chimane will not believe that you refused to come with me when she sees me alone. He agreed.

On the bus Dick told me much about his younger sister whom he was helping with money to stay at school until she finished; so that she could become a nurse and a midwife. He was very fond of her, as far as I could find out. He said he prayed always that he should not lose his job, as he had done many times before, after staying a few weeks only at each job; because of this he had to borrow monies from people to pay his sister's school fees, to buy her clothes and books. He spoke of her as if she were his sweetheart. She was clever at school, pretty (she was this in the photo Dick had shown me before). She was in Orlando Township. She looked after his old people, although she was only thirteen years of age. He said to me he said Today I still owe many people because I keep losing my job. You must try to stay with Mrs. Plum, I said.

I cannot say that I had all my mind on what Dick was telling me. I was thinking of Chimane: what could she be doing? Why that note?

We found her in bed. In that terrible township where night and day are full of knives and bicycle chains and guns and the barking of hungry dogs and of people in trouble. I held my heart in my hands. She was in pain and her face, even in the candlelight, was gray. She turned her eyes at me. A fat woman was sitting in a chair.

One arm rested on the other and held her chin in its palm. She had hardly opened the door for us after we had shouted our names when she was on her bench again as if there were nothing else to do.

She snorted, as if to let us know that she was going to speak. She said There is your friend. There she is my own-own niece who comes from the womb of my own sister, my sister who was made to spit out my mother's breast to give way for me. Why does she go and do such an evil thing. Ao! you young girls of today you do not know children die so fast these days that you have to thank God for sowing a seed in your womb to grow into a child. If she had let the child be born I should have looked after it or my sister would have been so happy to hold a grandchild on her lap, but what does it help? She has allowed a worm to cut the roots, I don't know.

Then I saw that Chimane's aunt was crying. Not once did she mention her niece by her name, so sore her heart must have been. Chimane only moaned.

Her aunt continued to talk, as if she was never going to stop for breath, until her voice seemed to move behind me, not one of the things I was thinking: trying to remember signs, however small, that could tell me more about this moment in a dim little room in a cruel township without street lights, near Chimane. Then I remembered the three-legged cat, its grey-green eyes, its *miau*. What was this shadow that seemed to walk about us but was not coming right in front of us?

I thanked the gods when Chimane came to work at the end of the week. She still looked weak, but that shadow was no longer there. I wondered Chimane had never told me about her aunt before. Even now I did not ask her.

I told her I told her white people that she was ill and had been fetched to Nokaneng by a brother. They would never try to find out. They seldom did, these people. Give them any lie, and it will do. For they seldom believe you whatever you say. And how can a black person work for white people and be afraid to tell them lies. They are always asking the questions, you are always the one to give the answers.

Chimane told me all about it. She had gone to a woman who did these things. Her way was to hold a sharp needle, cover the point with the finger, and guide it into the womb. She then fumbled in the womb until she found the egg and then pierced it. She gave you something to ease the bleeding. But the pain, spirits of our forefathers!

Mrs. Plum and Kate were talking about dogs one evening at dinner. Every time I brought something to table I tried to catch their words. Kate seemed to find it funny, because she laughed aloud. There was a word I could not hear well which began with *sem*—: whatever it was, it was to be for dogs. This I understood by putting a few words together. Mrs. Plum said it was something that was common in the big cities of America, like New York. It was also something Mrs. Plum wanted and Kate laughed at the thought. Then later I was to hear that Monty and Malan could be sure of a nice burial.

Chimane's voice came up to me in my room the next morning, across the fence. When I come out she tells me she says *Hei* child-of-my-father, here is something to tickle your ears. You know what? What? I say. She says, These white people can do things that make the gods angry. More godless people I have not seen. The madam of our house says the people of Greenside want to buy ground where they can bury their dogs. I heard them talk about it in the sitting room when I was giving them coffee last night. *Hei*, people, let our forefathers come and save us!

Yes, I say, I also heard the madam of our house talk about it with her daughter. I just heard it in pieces. By my mother one day these dogs will sit at table and use knife and fork. These things are to be treated like people now, like children who are never going to grow up.

Chimane sighed and she says *Hela batho*, why do they not give me some of that money they will spend on the ground and on gravestones to buy stockings! I have nothing to put on, by my mother.

Over her shoulder I saw the cat with three legs. I pointed with my head. When Chimane looked back and saw it she said *Hm*, even *they* live like kings. The mother-in-law found it on a chair and the madam said the woman should not drive it away. And there was no other chair, so the woman went to her room.

Hela!

I was going to leave when I remembered what I wanted to tell Chimane. It was that five of us had collected £1 each to lend her so that she could pay the woman of Alexandra for having done that thing for her. When Chimane's time came to receive money we collected each month and which we took in turns, she would pay us back. We were ten women and each gave £2 at a time. So one waited ten months to receive £20. Chimane thanked us for helping her.

I went to wake up Mrs. Plum as she had asked me. She was sleeping late this morning. I was going to knock at the door when I heard strange noises in the bedroom. What is the matter with Mrs. Plum? I asked myself. Should I call her, in case she is ill? No, the noises were not those of a sick person. They were happy noises but like those a person makes in a dream, the voice full of sleep. I bent a little to peep through the keyhole. What is this? I kept asking myself. Mrs. Plum! Malan! What is she doing this one? Her arm was round Malan's belly and pressing its back against her stomach at the navel, Mrs. Plum's body in a nightdress moving in jerks like someone in fits . . . her leg rising and falling . . . Malan silent like a thing to be owned without any choice it can make to belong to another.

The gods save me! I heard myself saying, the words sounding like wind rushing out of my mouth. So this is what Dick said I would find out for myself!

No one could say where it all started; who talked about it first; whether the police wanted to make a reason for

taking people without passes and people living with
servants and working in town or not working at all. But
the story rushed through Johannesburg that servants were
going to poison the white people's dogs. Because they
were too much work for us: that was the reason. We
heard that letters were sent to the newspapers by white
people asking the police to watch over the dogs to stop
any wicked things. Some said that we the servants were
not really bad, we were being made to think of doing
these things by evil people in town and in the locations.
Others said the police should watch out lest we poison
madams and masters because black people did not know
right from wrong when they were angry. We were still
children at heart, others said. Mrs. Plum said that she
had also written to the papers.

Then it was the police came down on the suburbs like
locusts on a cornfield. There were lines and lines of men
who were arrested hour by hour in the day. They liked
this very much, the police. Everybody they took, everybody who was working was asked, Where's the poison eh?
Where did you hide it? Who told you to poison the dogs
eh? If you tell us we'll leave you to go free, you hear? and
so many other things.

Dick kept saying It is wrong this thing they want to do
to kill poor dogs. What have these things of God done
to be killed for? Is it the dogs that make us carry passes?
Is it dogs that make the laws that give us pain? People
are just mad they do not know what they want, stupid!
But when white policeman spoke to him, Dick trembled
and lost his tongue and the things he thought. He just
shook his head. A few moments after they had gone
through his pockets he still held his arms stretched out,
like the man of straw who frightens away birds in a field.
Only when I hissed and gave him a sign did he drop his
arms. He rushed to a corner of the garden to go on with
his work.

Mrs. Plum had put Monty and Malan in the sitting
room, next to her. She looked very much worried. She

called me. She asked me she said Karabo, you think Dick
is a boy we can trust? I did not know how to answer. I
did not know whom she was talking about when she said
we. Then I said I do not know, Madam. You know! she
said. I looked at her. I said I do not know what Madam
thinks. She said she did not think anything, that was why
she asked. I nearly laughed because she was telling a lie
this time and not I.

At another time I should have been angry if she lied
to me, perhaps. She and I often told each other lies, as
Kate and I also did. Like when she came back from jail,
after that day when she turned a hosepipe on two policemen. She said life had been good in jail. And yet I could
see she was ashamed to have been there. Not like our
black people who are always being put in jail and only
look at it as the white man's evil game. Lilian Ngoyi often
told us this, and Mrs. Plum showed me how true those
words are. I am sure that we have kept to each other by
lying to each other.

There was something in Mrs. Plum's face as she was
speaking which made me fear her and pity her at the same
time. I had seen her when she had come from prison; I
had seen her when she was shouting at Kate and the girl
left the house; now there was this thing about dog poisoning. But never had I seen her face like this before. The
eyes, the nostrils, the lips, the teeth seemed to be full of
hate, tired, fixed on doing something bad; and yet there
was something on that face that told me she wanted me
on her side.

Dick is all right madam, I found myself saying. She
took Malan and Monty in her arms and pressed them to
herself, running her hands over their heads. They looked
so safe, like a child in a mother's arm.

Mrs. Plum said All right you may go. She said Do not
tell anybody what I have asked about Dick eh?

When I told Dick about it, he seemed worried.

It is nothing, I told him.

I had been thinking before that I did not stand with

those who wanted to poison the dogs, Dick said. But the police have come out, I do not care what happens to the dumb things, now.

I asked him I said Would you poison them if you were told by someone to do it?

No. But I do not care, he replied.

The police came again and again. They were having a good holiday, everyone could see that. A day later Mrs. Plum told Dick to go because she would not need his work any more.

Dick was almost crying when he left. Is madam so unsure of me? he asked. I never thought a white person could fear me! And he left.

Chimane shouted from the other yard. She said, *Hei ngoand'rona*, the boers are fire-hot eh!

Mrs. Plum said she would hire a man after the trouble was over.

A letter came from my parents in Phokeng. In it they told me my uncle had passed away. He was my mother's brother. The letter also told me of other deaths. They said I would not remember some, I was sure to know the others. There were also names of sick people.

I went to Mrs. Plum to ask her if I could go home. She asks she says When did he die? I answer I say It is three days, madam. She says So that they have buried him? I reply Yes Madam. Why do you want to go home then? Because my uncle loved me very much madam. But what are you going to do there? To take my tears and words of grief to his grave and to my old aunt, madam. No you cannot go, Karabo. You are working for me you know? Yes, madam. I, and not your people pay you. I must go madam, that is how we do it among my people, madam. She paused. She walked into the kitchen and came out again. If you want to go, Karabo, you must lose the money for the days you will be away. Lose my pay, madam? Yes, Karabo.

The next day I went to Mrs. Plum and told her I was leaving for Phokeng and was not coming back to her.

Could she give me a letter to say that I worked for her.
She did, with her lips shut tight. I could feel that something between us was burning like raw chillies. The letter
simply said that I had worked for Mrs. Plum for three
years. Nothing more. The memory of Dick being sent
away was still an open sore in my heart.

The night before the day I left, Chimane came to see
me in my room. She had her own story to tell me. Timi,
her boy-friend, had left her—for good. Why? Because I
killed his baby. Had he not agreed that you should do it?
No. Did he show he was worried when you told him you
were heavy? He was worried, like me as you saw me,
Karabo. Now he says if I kill one I shall eat all his children
up when we are married. You think he means what he
says? Yes, Karabo. He says his parents would have been
very happy to know that the woman he was going to
marry can make his seed grow.

Chimane was crying, softly.

I tried to speak to her, to tell her that if Timi left her
just like that, he had not wanted to marry her in the first
place. But I could not, no, I could not. All I could say
was Do not cry, my sister, do not cry. I gave her my
handkerchief.

Kate came back the morning I was leaving, from somewhere very far I cannot remember where. Her mother
took no notice of what Kate said asking her to keep me,
and I was not interested either.

One hour later I was on the Railway bus to Phokeng.
During the early part of the journey I did not feel anything about the Greenside house I had worked in. I was
not really myself, my thoughts dancing between Mrs.
Plum, my uncle, my parents, and Phokeng, my home. I
slept and woke up many times during the bus ride. Right
through the ride I seemed to see, sometimes in sleep,
sometimes between sleep and waking, a red car passing
our bus, then running behind us. Each time I looked out
it was not there.

Dreams came and passed. He tells me he says You have

killed my seed I wanted my mother to know you are a
woman in whom my seed can grow . . . Before you make
the police take you to jail make sure that it is for something big you should go to jail for, otherwise you will
come out with a heart and mind that will bleed inside
you and poison you . . .

The bus stopped for a short while, which made me
wake up.

The Black Crow, the club women . . . *Hei*, listen! I lie
to the madam of our house and I say I had a telegram
from my mother telling me she is very very sick. I show
her a telegram my sister sent me as if mother were writing.
So I went home for a nice weekend . . .

The laughter of the women woke me up, just in time
for me to stop a line of saliva coming out over my lower
lip. The bus was making plenty of dust now as it was
running over part of the road they were digging up. I was
sure the red car was just behind us, but it was not there
when I woke.

Any one of you here who wants to be baptized or has
a relative without a church who needs to be can come
and see me in the office . . . A round man with a fat
tummy and sharp hungry eyes, a smile that goes a long,
long way . . .

The bus was going uphill, heavily and noisily.

I kick a white man's dog, me, or throw it there if it
has not been told the black people's law . . . This is
Mister Monty and this is Mister Malan. Now get up you
lazy boys and meet Mister Kate. Hold out your hands and
say hallo to him . . . Karabo, bring two glasses there . . .
Wait a bit—What will you chew boys while Mister Kate
and I have a drink? Nothing? Sure?

We were now going nicely on a straight tarred road
and the trees rushed back. Mister Kate. What nonsense,
I thought.

Look Karabo, madam's dogs are dead. What? Poison.
I killed them. She drove me out of a job did she not? For
nothing. Now I want her to feel she drove me out for

something. I came back when you were in your room and took the things and poisoned them . . . And you know what? She has buried them in clean pink sheets in the garden. Ao, clean clean good sheets. I am going to dig them out and take one sheet do you want the other one? Yes, give me the other one I will send it to my mother . . . Hei, Karabo, see here they come. Monty and Malan. The bloody fools they do not want to stay in their hole. Go back you silly fools. Oh you do not want to move eh? Come here, now I am going to throw you in the big pool. No, Dick! No Dick! no, no! Dick! They cannot speak do not kill things that cannot speak. Madam can speak for them she always does. No! Dick. . . !

I woke up with a jump after I had screamed Dick's name, almost hitting the window. My forehead was full of sweat. The red car also shot out of my sleep and was gone. I remembered a friend of ours who told us how she and the garden man had saved two white sheets in which their white master had buried their two dogs. They went to throw the dogs in a dam.

When I told my parents my story Father says to me he says, So long as you are in good health my child, it is good. The worker dies, work does not. There is always work. I know when I was a boy a strong sound body and a good mind were the biggest things in life. Work was always there, and the lazy man could never say there was no work. But today people see work as something bigger than everything else, bigger than health, because of money.

I reply I say, Those days are gone Papa. I must go back to the city after resting a little to look for work. I must look after you. Today people are too poor to be able to help you.

I knew when I left Greenside that I was going to return to Johannesburg to work. Money was little, but life was full and it was better than sitting in Phokeng and watching the sun rise and set. So I told Chimane to keep her eyes and ears open for a job.

I had been at Phokeng for one week when a red car

arrived. Somebody was sitting in front with the driver, a
white woman. At once I knew it to be that of Mrs. Plum.
The man sitting beside her was showing her the way, for
he pointed towards our house in front of which I was
sitting. My heart missed a few beats. Both came out of
the car. The white woman said Thank you to the man
after he had spoken a few words to me.

I did not know what to do and how to look at her as
she spoke to me. So I looked at the piece of cloth I was
sewing pictures on. There was a tired but soft smile on
her face. Then I remembered that she might want to sit.
I went inside to fetch a low bench for her. When I remembered it afterwards, the thought came to me that
there are things I never think white people can want to
do at our homes when they visit for the first time: like
sitting, drinking water or entering the house. This is how
I thought when the white priest came to see us. One year
at Easter Kate drove me home as she was going to the
north. In the same way I was at a loss what to do for a
few minutes.

Then Mrs. Plum says, I have come to ask you to come
back to me, Karabo. Would you like to?

I say I do not know, I must think about it first.

She says, Can you think about it today? I can sleep at
the town hotel and come back tomorrow morning, and
if you want to you can return with me.

I wanted her to say she was sorry to have sent me away,
I did not know how to make her say it because I know
white people find it too much for them to say Sorry to a
black person. As she was not saying it, I thought of two
things to make it hard for her to get me back and maybe
even lose me in the end.

I say, You must ask my father first, I do not know,
should I call him?

Mrs. Plum says, Yes.

I fetched both Father and Mother. They greeted her
while I brought benches. Then I told them what she
wanted.

Father asks Mother and Mother asks Father. Father asks me. I say if they agree, I will think about it and tell her the next day.

Father says, It goes by what you feel my child.

I tell Mrs. Plum I say, if you want me to think about it I must know if you will want to put my wages up from £6 because it is too little.

She asks me, How much will you want?

Up by £4.

She looked down for a few moments.

And then I want two weeks at Easter and not just the weekend. I thought if she really wanted me she would want to pay for it. This would also show how sorry she was to lose me.

Mrs. Plum says, I can give you one week. You see you already have something like a rest when I am in Durban in the winter.

I tell her I say I shall think about it.

She left.

The next day she found me packed and ready to return with her. She was very much pleased and looked kinder than I had ever known her. And me, I felt sure of myself, more than I had ever done.

Mrs. Plum says to me, You will not find Monty and Malan.

Oh?

Yes, they were stolen the day after you left. The police have not found them yet. I think they are dead myself.

I thought of Dick . . . my dream. Could he? And she . . . did this woman come to ask me to return because she had lost two animals she loved?

Mrs. Plum says to me she says, You know, I like your people, Karabo, the Africans.

And Dick and Me? I wondered.